*A
Harlequin
Romance*

OTHER
Harlequin Romances
by ISOBEL CHACE

Many of these titles are available at your local bookseller,
or through the Harlequin Reader Service.

For a free catalogue listing all available Harlequin Romances,
send your name and address to:

HARLEQUIN READER SERVICE,
M.P.O. Box 707, Niagara Falls, N.Y. 14302
Canadian address: Stratford, Ontario, Canada.

or use order coupon at back of book.

THE DRAGON'S CAVE

by

ISOBEL CHACE

HARLEQUIN BOOKS   TORONTO
WINNIPEG

Original hard cover edition published in 1973
by Mills & Boon Limited.

© Isobel Chace 1973

SBN 373-01829-0

Harlequin edition published November 1974

Printed in Canada

CHAPTER I

Megan Meredith waited for the familiar clutch of nervousness that always seized her just before she stepped on to the stage. Supposing her voice failed? Supposing she tripped over her long skirt? Supposing Tony gave her the wrong beat and she didn't come in at the right place? It mattered more that evening than it had ever mattered, for her parents had come to hear her sing. She glanced over to where they were sitting, crouched over the tiny table that was lit by a single candle, looking the picture of discomfort mixed with despair.

For the first time Megan saw the room as they would see it. Dark, not particularly clean, the atmosphere laden with second-hand cigarette smoke, and the noise, amplified electronically, thudding out the beat to the detriment of the rhythm that was supposed to be supplied by the lead guitar.

The group, *her* group, was not the best available in London—she knew that without being told—but they were the only ones who had been prepared to give her an opening. They paid her very little, but they allowed her to sing with them and that, for the moment, was enough for her.

'—*the lovely Megan Meridith!*'

Megan took a step forward, flashed a smile round the room, trying not to look at her parents, and picked up the microphone. She had a soft, growly voice that was never going to be great, but which was charming and peculiarly feminine.

'Megan, my love, that was super!' Tony said, not to her but to the room, when she had come to the end of her song. 'We'll have to ask you again—say, in about ten minutes' time?'

She nodded her head, allowing the long length of

her loose hair to fall forward, hiding her face. Whatever her parents said, she knew that she was the best thing that had happened so far that evening. Even the rowdiest among them had stood silently listening to her, not even bothering to dance while she was singing. She wished if her parents would recognise the compliment they had paid her just by being quiet, but she knew that they wouldn't.

Megan went over to their table and sat on the free chair, her back as stiff as a ramrod.

'Well?' she said gruffly.

'Very nice, dear,' her father murmured, embarrassed.

Her mother merely looked at her, her eyes wide with dismay and—could it be *sympathy*?

'They listened to me, didn't they?' Megan went on abruptly.

'Meg, you're coming home with us *tonight*!' her mother decided.

'No,' Megan said firmly. 'I'm committed. I *want* to sing and this is the first opportunity I've had. It isn't much, I know, but it'll lead to better things.'

'When?'

'S-soon,' Megan stammered, sounding remarkably unsure.

'I don't believe it!' her mother retorted with all the confidence that her daughter had sought. 'We've argued about it quite long enough, Megan. You're coming home with us tonight!'

'You can't make me!' Megan said stubbornly, feeling unexpectedly childish.

'No,' her mother agreed, 'we can't make you. You're eighteen and you can do as you please. You can disappear and nobody will even look for you, presuming that you have enough sense to know what you're doing, if you want things that way. I don't think you're such a fool—'

'My dear,' Mr Meredith interrupted her nervously,

6

'I don't think you're putting this very well.'

'Megan and I understand one another,' Mrs Meredith said grimly. 'How often is this place raided?' she added meaningly.

Megan started. 'Raided?' she repeated.

'I'm sure it is,' her mother went on, her confidence verging on the arrogant. 'Next thing will be us having to bail you out on a drugs charge or something.'

'I d-don't smoke,' Megan reminded her.

Her mother smiled suddenly. 'Megan, don't be a fool,' she said softly. 'I understand that you want to sing, but this isn't the place for you. You wouldn't have hated your father and me coming here so much if it were!'

Megan wondered mutinously how her mother could have known how reluctant she had been to invite them to the Witch's Cauldron, as the small club was known. She bit her lip and their eyes met.

'All right, I'll come home,' Megan agreed dubiously. 'But I have to finish off tonight and, whatever you say, I *won't* settle for a secretarial course.'

Her mother actually grinned. 'I don't think anyone would employ you in an office anyway. You look as scatty as a hen with all that hair all over the place! And your idea of making up is enough to make an artist's palette shudder.'

Megan made a face at her. 'The lights are very dim in here,' she explained. 'I want to be seen!'

Her parents pushed back their chairs, exchanging looks of vivid relief that they were finally leaving.

'You don't have to hurry into anything, my dear,' her father said uncomfortably over his shoulder. 'I'm prepared to support you for a while yet until you get started decently.'

Megan pushed her hair back behind her ears. 'You don't understand!' she complained. 'I'm old enough to support myself! You'd have me accepting money from you until I'm doddering! And I *can* sing, whatever you think!'

'If it were only singing—' her father smiled at her. 'This place looks like a whole way of life. Is it yours?'

Megan shook her head, feeling near to tears. 'You've made your point!' she sighed. 'I'm coming home! Isn't that enough?'

Her father squeezed her arm. 'Anything you say,' he said gently.

Megan's eyes travelled to her mother's face. Her mother gave her a guilty look. 'We'll talk tomorrow,' she said. 'It's only because we love you very much, you know that! Darling, don't do anything *less* than the best you can. That's all we're asking!'

Megan threaded her fingers together. 'I've got to live my own life. I'm coming home when I've finished here, but I shan't give up trying to sing!'

'If that's what you want to do,' her mother agreed immediately.

'I do!' Megan insisted.

She watched her parents leave without getting up from her seat at the table. What else had she expected? she asked herself morosely. She had known that it would be a disaster to ask her parents to hear her sing. It was also something of a relief to know that after this one evening she would never have to see the inside of the Witch's Cauldron ever again.

She had gone to the party knowing that she would hate every minute of it. Alice, the girl who rented the flat above Tony's, had asked her to drop in and sing to her guests round about midnight, adding that the idea was to get rid of all the people that she didn't want to stay on into the small hours.

'Think you can do that?' she had asked Megan.

'I don't know,' Megan had said, wondering if she was complimented to be asked to sing after all.

'You have to wake them up, darling,' Alice had explained.

'I can do that,' Megan had said positively.

'Well then, no difficulty!' Alice had laughed.

And she had woken them up. She had sung her heart out, knowing that Tony was there and that he would hear her, and that he might think her good enough to sing with his group.

It had worked out exactly as she had hoped. Tony had heard her and he had asked her to sing. He had also kissed her as they had made their way down the stairs past his flat to the bus stop outside. Megan hadn't liked being kissed, but Tony had told her that it was expected of any girl singer to give as well as take, and at least she had gone home by herself on the bus.

The first night she had sung at the Witch's Cauldron, Tony had asked her to come along again.

'You have something,' he had told her. 'It's mostly your looks and the promise that you have something special to offer to anyone discerning enough to mine for it. Your voice is only pretty and different.'

'Is that good enough?' she had asked him, rather overawed at being summed up in such terms.

'If you play your cards right.'

She had worried about that quite a bit. 'I don't know—' she had said.

'Leave it to your Uncle Tony!'

Alice had come in with a friend later that evening. 'I don't think this is you,' she had said frankly to Megan. 'I suppose you know what you're doing?'

'Tony does!' her friend had said with a meaning look.

Alice had hesitated. 'Do you know about Tony?' she had asked Megan.

Megan had been plainly confused. Alice had shrugged her shoulders and had turned to her friend. 'You tell her, love!' she had commanded.

'Okay,' he had agreed. 'Tony eats little girls like you,' he had said, laughing. 'Run along home while you're still in one piece and welcome in the respectable neighbourhood where you were obviously brought up!'

Megan had thought him unkind. 'I can look after myself!' she had claimed defiantly.

'If you say so,' Alice had said, an edge to her voice. 'But do me a favour, will you? Ask your parents to come and hear you sing! It'll give them a fillip to know you're making out on your own.' She had turned away and smiled at her friend. 'I owe the Merediths something,' she had added meaningly. 'They used to take me out with Megan when we were at school together.'

Megan had wondered what she had found so funny about that, but she had done what Alice had suggested and had asked her parents and, in doing so, she had done herself out of a job.

She stepped out on to the platform for the last time. Tony was angry with her and he deliberately bruised her wrist with his fingers as he announced her. It was strange, she thought, that he should mind so much when he had thought she was worth so little to his group.

She sang a sad little protest song, her voice full of the tears she was longing to shed. Then she bowed, almost ran off the stage, came back and bowed again, hating the smell of stale cigarettes and stale beer that assaulted her nostrils. She felt quite sick and, without stopping to say anything to Tony, she pushed her way through the dancers and the small, crowded tables, up the stairs and into the cold night air. It was snowing, but she didn't care. It fell softly on her face, tickling her skin. It was very white and *clean*!

Megan didn't know how long she stood there, breathing in the cold air, but she did know that she resented Tony's presence when he stood in front of her, pushing a couple of pound notes into her hand.

'What's that for?' she asked with distaste.

'I'd like to say you earned it, but you didn't! You've ruined it for us all! They won't put up with us now without you!'

'I thought you were doing me a favour!' Megan sniffed.

'So I was! People as innocent as you shouldn't be allowed out on their own. I'd be doing mankind a favour to wake you up!'

'I don't know what you mean,' Megan said with dignity.

'I believe you!'

She winced, sure that he was referring to her youth and inexperience, neither of which could be immediately rectified, so she felt he had an unfair advantage.

'But you were working here before last night!' she reminded him wryly.

'That was before they heard you,' he retorted bitterly. 'Couldn't you feel the change that came over them? The guitars are okay, so far as they go, but you send them, honey, that's the difference!'

'I'm sorry,' she apologised.

'Heavens above! I should think you ought to be!' Megan shivered as a cold wind blew down the street. 'Yes, but—'

'Half the audience in there are men,' Tony went on harshly. 'I don't suppose *that* even occurred to you?'

'Why should it?' she responded sulkily.

He lifted his eyes to the skies. 'You're a pretty girl, my dear. Every man in the place would like to have you to themselves. I'm not above it myself!'

She gasped and blushed, wishing that she had more aplomb.

'Oh, but I—'

She felt his arms reach round her and his lips on hers. For an awful moment she thought she was going to be sick and told herself it was only the cold and the fright he had given her.

11

' Please, Tony!' she said when she could.

' You'll have to say please more prettily than that!'
he retorted. He kissed her again, ignoring the dry sobs
that shook her. ' What's the matter with you anyway?'
he demanded. ' Haven't you ever been kissed before?'

She didn't like to admit that she never had been, or
that she disliked it very much.

' Please, Tony,' she said again.

' You're a cold little piece, aren't you?' he muttered.
She shivered. ' It *is* snowing,' she stammered.

' All the more reason to warm up a bit!' He pulled
her even closer against him, his mouth closing once
again over hers. Megan turned her head away, but he
was too strong for her and she began to think she
would never escape him.

But no sooner had his lips met hers than a strong
arm came between them, forcing Tony away from her.
Megan turned away, leaning against a lamp-post, her
teeth chattering.

' Are you all right?' a deep, masculine voice asked
her. She thought she detected a foreign accent, but
she might just as easily have imagined it.

' No, I'm not!' she exclaimed frankly.

' It is hardly surprising,' the man went on, sounding
amused. ' Have you no coat on a night like this?'

' I came out for some fresh air.' She shuddered,
looking about her and surprised to discover that Tony
had gone. ' Wh-where's Tony?' she asked.

' The young man? He went into the Witch's
Cauldron. Are you with him?' He sounded disapproving.

' Not exactly. I was singing with his group, only
my parents came to hear me and they don't think I
should—'

' Where are your parents now?' he interrupted her.

' They went home. I promised I'd go home—to
their home, I mean—as soon as I finished here.'

' They would have been wiser to take you home

with them,' he observed.

'They couldn't! I—I had agreed to sing tonight, you see.'

'I'm not sure that I do,' he said gently, and she was quite sure now that he was a foreigner, though he spoke English very well. 'Where do you live? I will fetch your coat for you and then I will take you home.'

She glared at him suspiciously. The orange light was enough to make anyone look ill and ghostly, but he stood up to it surprisingly well. His hair was jet black, and he was tall and thin, with expensive clothes and a solid gold watch of the sort that you never have to wind.

Megan put a hand up to her hair and pushed it back behind her shoulders. 'I must look a mess,' she said, blinking up at him.

'You will be quite safe with me,' he assured her.

'Oh?'

He smiled. 'I think you are too young to be a temptation to me,' he said smoothly. 'You should be tucked up in bed at this hour!'

'I'm not all that young!' she said, stung.

'You look very young to me,' he returned with quiet certainty. He put a hand under her chin, turning her face up to the light. 'Only the very young would wear everything in the make-up box all at once!'

She twisted away from him. 'The lights aren't very good in the Witch's Cauldron!'

'I see,' he said casually.

She wondered just what it was that he did see. 'It—it was kind of you to rescue me from—from Tony,' she said gravely. 'He took me by surprise, you see, or it would never have happened. But there's no need for you to do anything further. I'll fetch my coat and then I'll go home, so you see I shall be quite all right.'

'Nevertheless, I should prefer to see you safely home.'

She looked at him curiously. 'Why?'

He shrugged his shoulders. 'Shall I come in with you to fetch your coat?' he asked her.

She shook her head, but he came in with her just the same. He stood just inside the entrance, looking about the place with an arrogant expression of distaste. Megan noticed that the waiters were all immediately aware of his presence and that almost everyone looked his way. She felt suddenly proud that he was with her, even if it wasn't exactly true, because he was so supremely unaware of the effect he had, on her as much as on anybody else.

'I shan't be a moment,' she told him.

'I will wait,' he answered simply.

Megan took the opportunity to take a look at herself in the looking glass and was dismayed to find that her mascara had run into her tears and that she looked a mess. She turned on a tap and scrubbed her face with a paper handkerchief until it was gleaming. She made a face at herself in the glass and searched in her handbag for her lipstick, applying it carefully to her lips. Without her false eyelashes and her eye-shadow, she looked younger than ever, but she didn't like to keep the tall stranger waiting any longer, so she hurried out to join him.

He was talking to Tony, listening courteously to some lengthy explanation from the younger man. He saw Megan immediately and excused himself politely, moving easily towards her.

'Are you ready?' he asked her.

'I wish you wouldn't bother—' she began again.

'That's what I was telling him,' Tony put in. 'I can see you home, Megan.'

She repressed a shudder, taking a step closer to the stranger. 'No!' she said flatly.

'I didn't mean anything,' Tony said crossly.

'I know,' she managed. 'I expect it was partly my fault.'

'It was!' Tony assured her dryly.

'Are you now warmer?' the stranger put in casually. 'If you are, I think we had better go now.'

Megan smiled up at him. 'Yes, let's go,' she said.

'When will I see you again?' Tony asked plaintively as they made their way through the door.

'Another time,' the stranger answered him curtly. 'This is no place for a young lady to be at this hour of night.'

'She's a *singer*!' Tony laughed.

'So she has told me,' the stranger said flatly. 'It is not what I would choose for any young relative of mine—'

'But I do sing,' Megan confirmed eagerly.

'That is something I shall speak to your parents about. Now you will please tell me their address and I shall take you home."

At another time, she would have resented his arrogance, but now all she could feel was relief that she didn't have to see Tony again and that she didn't have to struggle home by herself on the suburban trains at that time of night.

'My parents live in Kent. If you'll see me to Victoria Station—'

'I prefer to take you home.'

She blinked. 'But it will take you *ages*!'

'We will take the car,' he answered simply. 'My hotel is not far from here. Do you mind walking a short distance?'

She shook her head. 'I'm sorry to be a nuisance,' she said in a small voice. 'But you don't have to go to so much trouble.'

'I know I don't.'

'Then—then why?' she asked.

'Because I choose to do so,' he said unanswerably.

She walked beside him in silence for a long moment. 'I don't even know your name,' she objected. 'I'm Megan Meredith.'

'Megan?' he repeated. 'I have not heard this name

before. Is it English?'

'Welsh,' she said.

He pulled his coat closer about him against the still falling snow. 'That is why you sing?' he suggested.

'I suppose so,' she admitted.

'I am Carlos Vallori Llobera.'

'Oh,' she said.

'I am Spanish,' he added unnecessarily.

'You look Spanish,' she told him.

'I do?' He sounded surprised.

She wished she hadn't spoken. 'You're so tall,' she said by way of explanation.

'Like Don Quixote?'

His pronunciation of the name was strange to her and it was a moment before she realised whom he meant. 'I suppose so,' she said.

'I am more like him than Sancho, don't you think?' he said.

She chuckled. 'Yes, you are. I can't imagine you riding on a mule!'

'Why not?' he countered.

'No, no, it would have to be a very fine horse to look right!'

He raised his eyebrows thoughtfully. 'So?'

'Yes, of course!' she went on impatiently. 'A mule would be far too humble a mount for you!'

He frowned at her. 'Are you always so indiscreet in your remarks?' he cautioned her.

She bit her lip. 'I'm sorry,' she said.

'Are you?'

'I didn't mean to tease you,' she added. 'Only you must see that you'd look better on a horse than on a mule?'

'I am sure I should,' he agreed. 'What I meant was that it is easy to see why this young man of yours thought you wanted his attentions.'

'I don't see why,' she said. 'I hardly know him.'

'You hardly know me,' he pointed out.

Megan gave him a mystified look. 'I don't know what you're talking about,' she said gruffly.

He laughed out loud. 'I am telling you that it is unwise to flatter unknown males when you are alone with them,' he reproved her. 'It may lead to other undesirable incidents.'

She felt herself blushing. 'I wasn't flattering you!' she denied.

'No?' He dismissed the matter easily, pointing out his hotel to her. 'I will fetch the car,' he told her. 'You will be quite safe here, in the light from the hotel.'

'Yes,' she agreed mechanically.

'You are not nervous of the dark?' he probed.

She was, but she had no intention of admitting such a weakness to him.

'No.'

'Good.' He gave her a long, grave look and then walked away from her, down some side street, leaving her on her own with the snow fluttering down around her.

She didn't know why she was letting him drive her to her parents' home. The fact that he was tall and elegant, and never for a moment considered that she might refuse to fall in with his arrangements, had nothing to do with it. She had argued with better men, she told herself, even if they hadn't been as arrogant as this Spaniard. Perhaps it was just that she liked the feeling, after all, of some knight in shining armour carrying her away into the winter night. He looked the part for that, she thought. Haughty and unbending and full of Spanish honour! She had never met anyone quite like him before and he intrigued her, though how she was going to explain him away to her parents, she simply could not imagine.

For a knight, his charger, in the shape of an extremely expensive-looking Mercedes car, was a delight to behold. Megan slipped into the front seat beside him, rejoicing in the warmth that enveloped her. It gave her a queer feeling to be on the right side of the car, but she supposed that was because he usually drove in Spain and not in England.

'Where to?' he asked briefly.

She swallowed, once more aware of how very far she was taking him, a stranger, out of his way. 'Tunbridge Wells,' she said.

He didn't appear to be surprised, or particularly concerned.

'Do you return there every night?' he asked her.

She shook her head. 'I share a room with a friend.'

He raised his eyebrows. 'And this friend, does she have charge of you?'

Megan giggled. 'Good heavens, no! We were at school together. Alice—I was at school with her too—found it for us. It's fairly near her place. We were all going to share with her, but she—it wasn't convenient,' she ended lamely, hoping that he wouldn't ask her why.

'Is she, too, as young as you?'

Megan grinned at him. 'We're all of age!' she said, rather smugly.

'You too?' His disbelief was obvious.

'I'm eighteen!' she exclaimed.

'That is no age at all,' he snubbed her. 'One of my sisters is also eighteen, but I should not dream of allowing her to run round Madrid, or London, on her own! If you had an unpleasant experience this evening, it was no more than to be expected—'

'Tony didn't mean anything!' Megan protested.

The Spaniard gave her an impatient look. 'I find it shocking that young women should be left defenceless to deal with young men who don't mean anything,' he said brutally.

'Isn't that rather old-fashioned?' she retorted.

'Not at all. Some kinds of behaviour are a matter of taste rather than fashion.'

18

Crushed, Megan sought to explain herself. 'Alice introduced me to Tony,' she began.

'And this Alice? Is she a respectable person?'

Megan doubted that he would consider Alice respectable in any way. 'She's nice,' she compromised.

'But not respectable?'

Megan thought of the men Alice knew and then with relief of the man she had decided to marry, a man with a title and an ex-wife lurking somewhere in the background.

'She's marrying very well,' she said defensively.

The Spaniard glared at the snow falling on the road ahead of him.

'She would not in Spain!' he claimed grandly and with finality. Megan, stealing a look at his autocratic countenance, could well believe him. But then neither she nor Alice were living in Spain.

CHAPTER II

Megan never knew what the Spaniard said to her parents. She had spent a fruitless few minutes in the driveway of her parents' home trying to persuade him that her mother and father would have gone to bed long since and that the last thing they would appreciate was being disturbed at that hour. He had not listened at all.

' I think they will wish to see me,' he had said firmly. ' They will want to assure themselves that you are home and they will also be interested in something else I have to say to them.'

' Something else?'

' It will be better if you go straight to bed,' he had gone on. ' You must be tired after all your adventures.'

' You mean I look awful?' she had retorted crossly.

He had switched on the light in the car by opening his door and had taken a good look at her.

' No, not awful,' he had said kindly. ' But very young and very tired.'

' That means the same thing!' Megan had sighed, hurt.

' No. To look young is charming. Before you washed your face you looked awful, but not now.'

She had blushed, suddenly aware of his dark eyes studying her face. ' I didn't wash for you!' she had insisted sharply. ' I *never* wear much make-up except when I'm performing!'

He had got out of the car without further comment and had gone up to the front door, firmly ringing the bell although she had kept on telling him that she had a key of her own. When her father had come to the door, the collar of his dressing-gown all awry, the Spaniard had touched her cheek with a finger and had pointed up the stairs.

'Goodnight, Megan Meredith,' he had said.

Megan had looked to her father for support, but he had looked so astonished at the sight of his visitor that Megan had known that he was not at all interested in her reactions.

'But—' she had begun by way of protest.

'Goodnight, niña!'

She had resented the endearment—at least she had supposed it was an endearment—almost as much as his imperious tone of voice.

'Goodnight, señor!' she had answered crossly. She had started up the stairs, pausing as soon as she had thought she was out of sight.

'Señorita?' his voice had carried up to her. 'You want something?'

'No!' she had denied. 'Nothing at all!'

Megan had listened in vain for some protest from her father, but apparently he had made none. Disconsolate, she had gone to her room, thinking how much she disliked her Spanish rescuer, but when she had slept, she had dreamed about him and in her dreams she had not disliked him at all.

It was inevitable that she had overslept the next morning. She had meant to be the first one downstairs and to have taken her mother her breakfast in bed, but when she opened her eyes it was gone ten o'clock and the blue light on the ceiling had told her immediately that the snow had come to stay.

Megan hurried out of bed, pulling on jeans and a sweater, and rushed down the stairs as fast as she could. Her mother was in the kitchen and she called out to her as she went past in search of her father.

'Megan!'

She wondered briefly whether she should ignore her mother's commanding voice, deciding that she had better not. She went reluctantly back to the kitchen.

'Sit down, Megan,' her mother ordered.

I want to go and look at the snow,' said Megan.

' Your father and I want to talk to you—'

' It's all right, Mother. I won't be going back to the Witch's Cauldron. I don't think Tony would have me back anyway.'

' I'm glad to hear it,' her mother said dryly.

' Yes, but one has to begin somewhere!' Megan burst out.

Her mother looked at her, an odd expression in her eyes. ' I like your Spaniard,' she said irrelevantly. ' He's coming to lunch today.'

' But we don't *know* him!'

' Now, Megan, he took a lot of trouble on your behalf last night. He's quite right too when he says that you shouldn't be on your own in London at your age. We've worried about you quite a bit recently and we should have done something about it—'

Megan glanced up with startled eyes. 'He had the *effrontery*—'

' He was right,' her mother interrupted firmly.

' I can look after myself!'

' Famous last words!' her mother jeered lightly. ' He wouldn't say how or where he came across you last night, but it didn't sound as though you were making out very well at that moment.'

Megan flushed. ' I was already convinced about the Witch's Cauldron. I had agreed to come home, hadn't I? What right has he, a total stranger, to interfere with what I do?'

Her mother sighed. ' He's bringing his sister with him today.'

' I shall go out!' Megan declared.

' You will not,' her father said quietly from the kitchen door. ' He was kind enough to bring you home yesterday and you will be here to thank him for that.'

Megan subsided into her chair, defeated. ' But don't you *mind* that he should lecture you about me?'

To her surprise, both her parents laughed.

' Well?' she demanded hotly.

' No, we didn't mind,' her mother said mildly. ' To tell the truth he was something of a relief to us—'

Her parents exchanged glances and laughed again.

' Quite a relief!' her father said with feeling.

' I don't see why,' Megan objected.

' He's not just coming to lunch,' her mother explained. ' He has a suggestion to make to you. That's why he's bringing his sister with him.'

' What suggestion?' Megan asked hollowly.

' He prefers to tell you himself,' her father answered easily.

Megan stared at them both in complete astonishment. For the last year or so she and her parents had indulged in a kind of entrenched warfare whenever they had been together, they disapproving of everything she did, she disliking the restraints they had tried to impose on her. But they had never relinquished a jot of their parental right to criticise her to anyone else before, and it wasn't even that they knew anything about the Spaniard!

' He doesn't approve of me,' she said uneasily. ' He thinks I should be closeted at home until some man comes along and deigns to marry me. And what's more,' she added on a rising note of indignation, ' he thinks you should be doing the closeting!'

' Is that wrong?' her father asked reasonably.

' It's archaic!' Megan commented graphically.

' Well, I think he's right,' said her father. ' We shouldn't have allowed you to take off for London on your own.'

' Why not?'

' Alice,' her father said flatly.

' *Alice?*' echoed Megan.

' She's never been a good influence and I don't like the people she's introduced you to in London—'

Megan blinked. ' What's wrong with them?'

' I think you know,' her father answered steadily.

'But *I'm* not like that! I'm not silly!'

'No, but you're young. Enough said, Megan. I prefer the ideas of this Spaniard of yours.'

'Well, I don't!' Megan retorted mutinously.

'You haven't heard them yet,' her mother pointed out gently. She looked out of the window at the snow-covered garden. 'I thought you wanted to go out and look at the snow?'

'Making a snowman?' her father asked, grinning.

Megan shrugged her shoulders, not entirely mollified by this change of subject. 'I might,' she said, her voice still prickly.

'I'll give you a hand,' Mr Meredith offered.

Megan smiled suddenly and held out her hand to him. 'Okay, you're on!' she agreed. 'But you're not to give up halfway through because you're cold like you did last time! This one has got to be finished properly!'

Her father grunted. 'That's right, blame me! Who was the one complaining of frostbite that's what I'd like to know!'

Still grumbling, he climbed into his thick winter coat and accompanied her out of the back door and down the slippery garden path, prodding at the deep snow with the toe of his wellington boot to make sure he wasn't trampling over one of the flower beds in error.

Inevitably Megan did most of the work. She set to with a will, as determined in this as she was in everything else, piling the snow up higher and higher.

'If you make him much taller you won't be able to reach the top of his head,' Mr Meredith objected, contenting himself with standing and watching her.

Megan cast him a look filled with mischief. 'I want to make him as tall as Señor Carlos Vallori Llobera!'

'So you know his name, then?'

'Of course,' she said. 'Didn't you?'

Her father chuckled. '*Touché.* I never can get the hang of foreign names. I'll get him to write it down for me some time and learn it from that!'

'Why bother?' Megan asked languidly.

'I think I'll be hearing it again pretty often in the future,' her father answered. 'He's that sort of man.'

Megan lifted enquiring eyebrows. 'What did you talk about last night?'

'That would be telling!'

'I don't think it's nice to talk about people behind their backs,' she observed reprovingly.

'Tell that to him!' her father recommended.

'I will,' Megan said grimly. 'I have a lot to say to that man!'

But her father only laughed. 'I daresay he'll have something to say to you!'

Megan was unexpectedly nervous at the thought. He had only seen her in the dark and he hadn't thought much of her then. 'Perhaps I'd better change,' she said aloud. 'Perhaps I'll wear—no, I can't! I left it in London. I haven't *anything* fit to wear down here!'

'I don't see anything wrong with your trousers,' Mr Meredith put in.

'If they *were* trousers!' Megan said scornfully. 'But they're *jeans*! *And* I've had them since I was fourteen. 'Bout what they look like!'

'About what you look like!' her father teased her.

Megan tossed a snowball at his head, knowing that he hated it when the snow crumbled and ran down the back of his neck.

'You behave like it too!' he complained, shaking his fist at her and making her giggle. 'In fact I think you were more grown up when you were fourteen!'

She made a face at him. 'Only because you knew where I was—at school!'

'I used to worry about you then because you wouldn't do any work. I didn't know I was in clover!'

Megan bit her lip. 'Have you really been worried about me?' she asked tentatively.

'Not as much as I should have been, but enough. I'll be better pleased when you're settled—'

'Settled? I suppose you want to marry me off to someone suitable?'

'Not just yet,' her father teased her. 'I'll put up with worrying about you for a little longer!'

She threw another snowball in his direction, missed him, and watched it land with a plop behind him. She gathered up some more snow, patting it firmly together, so intent on what she was doing that she failed to hear the approaching car, or the sound of the car door opening. She turned suddenly and cast the snowball where her father had been standing, but her father had gone over to the car. The snowball arched a curve into the sky and fell inexorably on the back of the Spaniard's head.

'Oh!' Megan gasped.

He turned and saw her, strode across the garden, stooping suddenly to scoop up some snow. His aim was better than hers, the snowball hitting her straight in the face.

'*Oh!*' she repeated furious.

'That has given you a fine colour!' he smiled at her.

'Better than paint!' she retorted sharply.

His eyebrows flew upwards. 'Did I hurt your feelings?' he enquired.

'Of course not,' she said.

'I think I did. I'm sorry.' He studied her face thoughtfully. 'You're a very pretty girl.'

'Thank you, kind sir!' She reddened as he went on looking at her. 'I—I was just going inside to change.'

'Were you? Come and meet my sister first. I brought her specially down to meet you.'

Megan would have liked to have asked him why, but something in his expression prevented her. In the full light of day, his hair looked blacker than ever and the arrogant lines of his face were etched deeper than she had thought. His eyes were not brown as she had expected, but the dark green of the leaf of the Spanish oak tree.

'Señor,' she began, and stopped.

'Yes?'

'Thank you for bringing me home last night. It was—kind of you.'

He looked surprised. 'I thought you resented me?'

'I prefer not to be discussed behind my back,' she said roundly, her gratitude forgotten.

'I have no intention of doing so,' he assured her. 'That is why I have come to luncheon with your family today.' He took her hand in his and walked with her back to the car.

Megan had been conscious of her mud-stained jeans before, but it was nothing to how she felt when the Spaniard's sister stepped out of the car, grimacing faintly as her pretty shoes became embedded in the snow. She was the loveliest girl Megan had ever seen. Her hair, as black as her brother's, was worn ballerina style, accentuating her long neck and the elegant slant of her shoulders. She was dressed in a scarlet velvet coat, edged in black, and carried a muff of snow-white fur that she hugged to her against the cold.

'You are Megan?' she asked, her English accent impeccable. 'It is you we have come to see?'

Megan nodded. 'Won't you come inside, señorita? It's cold today, but it's quite warm in the house.'

The Spanish girl smiled. 'Not señorita, please! I am Pilar Vallori. Please call me Pilar?'

'Thank you,' Megan said. 'Vallori Llobera?'

Pilar giggled infectiously. 'No, that is Carlos,' she answered. 'His mother was a Llobera—a very grand family, I'll have you know! Mine was a Hudson before she married.' She ran into the house, shaking her feet like a cat as she went. 'Vallori Hudson doesn't sound quite the same, does it?'

'You're half English!' Megan discovered.

Pilar nodded happily. 'But I am very Spanish about the English winter,' she said. 'How do you endure it?'

Megan grinned. 'Quite easily,' she said. 'I even like it when it looks pretty and new as it does today.'

Pilar laughed, peeling off various layers of outer clothes as she did so.

'I am so happy to be here!' she exclaimed. 'Carlos says you are the answer to our prayers, and now that I've seen you I can quite believe it!'

'Me?' Megan said in disbelief.

'You're just the person!'

'For what?' Megan asked.

Pilar's eyes twinkled mischievously. 'It isn't long since my father died,' she said by way of explanation. 'My mother went to pieces and is only beginning to recover now. She wants to come and live in England—'

'It's natural she should want to be with her own people,' Megan interposed.

'She hasn't got any!' Pilar said cheerfully. 'Only us!'

'Oh, I see,' said Megan, more mystified than ever.

'Anyway, Carlos says she'll only be more miserable than ever on her own and it's so difficult moving money about from one country to another. She might not be comfortable or able to have all she wants, or she won't be able to find a maid, or something devastating like that, and then what would she do?'

Megan blinked. 'A maid?' she repeated.

'You see,' Pilar went on sagely, 'if she had lived all her life in England, she would be used to managing things in the English way, but she's been living in Spain for *twenty* years! Papa simply doted on her, of course, and she never had to lift a finger in the house. Now, I don't suppose she'd know how!'

'Oh,' said Megan again.

'Carlos says—' Pilar began, and stopped. 'No, I'd better not say that. Carlos will want to tell you himself. I wasn't sure when he first said he'd met you, but now I've seen you, I'm all for the idea! Mama will love it!'

'Love what?' Megan asked blankly.

'Carlos will tell you!' Pilar said mysteriously. She looked curiously about her. 'How did you meet Carlos? He wouldn't tell me anything about how you met! Not that he ever tells me anything anyway.'

Megan was amused. 'I don't suppose he tells anyone much,' she said.

'No,' Pilar agreed bitterly. 'If you're going upstairs to change, may I come with you?'

It was Megan's first experience of the Spanish habit of doing everything together. Pilar sat on her bed and admired her possessions as naturally as if she had known her all her life. Megan, who was used to doing things on her own, soon began to realise that Pilar, on the other hand, was hardly ever alone. If she went out, her mother or a friend accompanied her. If she visited another member of her family, someone would take her and collect her or, on the rare occasions when she used public transport, the entire family would turn out to buy her ticket and to cheer her on her way, providing chocolates and magazines and other tokens of affection, no matter how short the journey.

'What are you going to wear?' Pilar asked curiously, obviously dying to peek into Megan's wardrobe.

'I haven't much here,' Megan answered.

'No?' Pilar sounded surprised. 'Then where are all your clothes?'

'In London. I share a bed-sitter with another girl.'

'*By yourself?*'

'Why not?' asked Megan.

'Carlos would never allow me to live anywhere but at home,' Pilar sighed. 'I think you are very lucky!'

Megan smiled. 'I suppose so,' she said uncertainly. 'It's a bit lonely sometimes. The girl-friend I share with does temporary work and she's away almost as much as she's there.'

'But you must get lonely!' Pilar exclaimed sympathetically. 'Perhaps you have your family near by?'

Megan shook her head. 'I have another school friend who lives a couple of streets away, but—' She trailed off, not knowing quite how to explain about Alice and her own natural reluctance to visit her very often.

'She is affianced, I expect?' Pilar put in.

'Something like that,' Megan agreed thankfully.

Pilar gave her a naughty look. 'Ah! You do not *approve* of her, but you like her a little. Do your parents know? Mine would blow a fuse if they knew I was going about with anyone like that!'

Megan couldn't help laughing. 'I don't know if they know or not,' she admitted.

'Life is very unfair,' Pilar went on with feeling. 'Carlos knows many people, women, who are not *quite* respectable, but he doesn't allow me to know any at all!'

'How do you know that he knows them?' Megan asked, a little put out that Carlos should have another standard for himself than the one he applied to other people.

'I know!' Pilar replied unanswerably. 'Women gossip—you know how it is! Wives hear things from their husbands and soon we all know! Many of my mother's friends would like to marry their daughters to Carlos, so all his affairs are reviewed often. Mama finds it very amusing because they used to do exactly the same when Papa's first wife died. Only then she didn't know that he was going to marry *her*, you understand. She thought he would marry someone important again, like Carlos' mother, but he fell in love with her.'

Megan struggled into the dress of her choice, a soft woollen dress of palest apricot that looked well with her light brown hair.

'I suppose Carlos will marry someone important too?' she suggested, pulling at the waist to make it sit better.

'*Absolutamente si!* Carlos is very proud. Mama teases him a little about it, but I think she likes it really. Carlos is the image of Papa, much more like him than any of us!'

'How many brothers and sisters have you?' Megan asked.

'Besides Carlos, there is Pepe, who is in South America, and Isabel, and me. Isabel is seventeen, I am nearly nineteen, and Pepe is twenty-one.'

Megan swallowed. 'There must be quite a gap between him and Carlos?' she queried. 'He looks much older!'

'Nearly thirty,' Pilar confirmed. She gave Megan an appreciative look, admiring her typically English looks. 'Do you always wear your hair that way? In Spain, we seldom wear it loose like that, unless we are very young. I like it. It suits you very well. But you know that! Heaps of people will have told you so!'

'Hardly anyone,' Megan said a little sadly. 'They'll be wondering where we are. Shall we go downstairs?'

Pilar danced down the stairs with eager steps, almost colliding with her brother in the hall.

'Carlos!' she exclaimed, well pleased. 'See how pretty Megan looks in this dress? Will you tell her *now*?'

The Spaniard looked up the stairs towards Megan, his eyes dark and enigmatic. 'Did you borrow the dress?' he asked her. 'It seems a little big for you.'

Megan made a face. 'I must have lost weight in the last few weeks,' she admitted.

He shook his head at her. 'You are too thin,' he told her abruptly.

She froze, her head held high. 'I don't think that's any business of yours!'

He put up a hand and guided her down the last few

31

stairs so that she had to give up the advantage she had had of looking down on him. Now he could look down on her.

'Let's go into the sitting room,' he said gently.

'You are going to ask her now!' Pilar crowed happily. 'Oh, Carlos, may I come too? I want to see her face when you tell her! It's such a brilliant idea!'

'No, you may not,' the Spaniard said firmly. To Megan's surprise, Pilar didn't press the point, but went meekly away towards the kitchen where Megan could hear her mother preparing the lunch.

'I don't know why you have to be so secretive,' Megan said crossly. 'I think it's rather silly, if you want to know!'

'I wanted to be sure that my stepmother would like you,' he answered callously. 'It was hard to tell last night. She would have to approve of you first, but as Pilar likes you, she will be well disposed towards you.'

Megan bit her lip. She longed to tell him that the approval or otherwise of his family meant nothing at all to her, but something prevented her. She wished that somehow Carlos had met her under other circumstances, circumstances that she could be proud of, instead of the shame that gripped her whenever it was mentioned, not, she thought, because it had been Tony who had kissed her, but because it had been this Spaniard, with his funny, old-fashioned ideas, who had discovered her being kissed by Tony.

'Pilar says her mother wants to live in England,' she put in hastily, hoping to turn the conversation away from herself.

Carlos dismissed the idea with a gesture. 'It crossed her mind, but she sees that it is impracticable,' he said firmly. 'How often would she see her family, with all of them living in Barcelona? She would die of loneliness! No, I have told her that she will be better off living in the family houses in Mallorca. There are enough English people there for her to feel at home,' he added dryly, 'and I have promised that she shall have an English companion.'

'But won't her daughters be with her?' Megan objected.

'They have to finish their education. They will stay with an aunt in Barcelona for the next year. I shall be able to keep an eye on them because I am there a good deal myself.'

'But your mother—'

'My stepmother is English.' Carlos looked suddenly amused. 'Actually she is not at all English! She depended completely on my father and now that he is gone she doesn't know what to do with herself! She has very little of this independence that the English admire in their women.'

Megan stole a look at him to see if he was joking, but he looked perfectly serious. 'What do you want me to do?' she asked uneasily.

'I want you to go to Mallorca with my stepmother, to look after her and keep her company, until Pilar and Isabel are free to live with her. She will not be so lonely if she has someone young around the house and, for you, it will be a pleasant place in which to grow into a woman—'

'I won't do it!'

His eyebrows rose. 'You have not considered—'

'No! *You* haven't considered!' Megan said passionately. 'I'm a singer, not a—a maid of all work! I *want* to sing!'

Carlos looked severe and his eyes were full of disapproval. 'It is unlikely that any of the young men you meet will be any more interested in your *voice* than that Tony of yesterday was,' he said dryly.

'I might have known that you'd say something beastly!' Megan stormed at him, her colour high.

'It is the truth,' he went on in the same, clipped tones. 'This singing can have no importance in your life, Megan. In time you will marry and have children, what use will your singing in places like the Witch's Cauldron be to you then?'

'It's important to me!' Megan declared. 'There are other places! They aren't all like the Witch's Cauldron!'

His lips twitched. 'With you cast as the Witch?' She was hurt. 'I wasn't!'

'No, you looked very young. Too young to be trying to sing sophisticated songs to such people.' He looked squarely into her eyes, forcing her to meet his eyes by sheer force of will. 'Did you like to know the thoughts that were going through their heads about you?' he demanded ruthlessly.

Megan swallowed, unable to reply.

'Well?' he pressed her.

'No,' she admitted. 'But why should you make a job for me? I'm nothing to you!'

Carlos grinned. 'I am sure Pilar has told you already that you are the answer to our united prayers,' he said with sudden humour. 'My stepmother is no sinecure, I can assure you of that. So you will go to Mallorca and be kind to her?'

Megan stared at him, searching for the right words with which to refuse him in a way he couldn't possibly misunderstand, because of course she wasn't going to do anything of the sort!

'If you want me to,' she said.

CHAPTER III

Megan could have bitten out her tongue.

'I—I mean—'

'*Muy bien!* It is all settled, then? Naturally, I shall pay your salary in whichever currency you prefer. You may prefer half in pesetas and half in sterling? You will not need much money in Mallorca. My stepmother is still in mourning—she is old-fashioned in these ways—and does not go out a great deal.'

'I see,' said Megan.

'I hope you will not find it dull. Pilar and Isabel will be there for their holidays, but otherwise there will not be a great deal for you to do.'

Megan listened to him explaining exactly what she would be called upon to do, her mind racing as she wondered whatever could have induced her to have given way to him. She was secretly amused, too, that he should be so concerned that she might be bored. Didn't he know, she wondered, how lonely it could be in the heart of swinging London, when you knew few people and had very little money?

'We have two houses in Mallorca,' he went on. 'One is in Palma itself, just off the Plaza Santa Eulalia, in the Calle Morey. It is a typical Mallorcan house and my stepmother is fond of it. She and my father spent some of their honeymoon there. The other house is on the east side of the island. We grow almonds and export them and this house is in the centre of the orchards.' His expression relaxed a little. 'You are fortunate to be going at this time of year,' he said gently. 'The blossom is very fine in the early part of February.'

'Is your stepmother already there?' Megan asked him.

'She goes there tomorrow,' he answered. 'How soon

can you be ready to join her?'

Megan shrugged. She thought of saying that after all, she didn't want to go, but she couldn't bring herself to do it.

' I—I can be ready as soon as I've packed,' she said instead. ' Most of my things are in London, but I can go and get them tomorrow.'

' Fine. I shall collect you on Tuesday, the day after tomorrow. There will be no difficulty in getting a seat on a plane at this time of year. I shall telephone my stepmother tonight and tell her that you are coming.'

He stood up, offering her his hand to clinch their bargain. Reluctantly, she put her hand in his, wishing that he didn't make her feel quite so young and foolish. To her surprise, he didn't shake her hand as she had expected, but raised it to his lips, kissing it lightly.

' I thought Spaniards didn't kiss the hands of unmarried ladies?' she said nervously.

' Do you object?' he countered.

' N-no,' she said. She thought she would sound even more young and foolish if she said she did. ' I just wondered if it were quite proper.'

His dark green eyes glinted with laughter. ' Quite proper, seeing the difference in our ages—'

' You aren't thirty yet!' she reproved him.

He sighed. ' Pilar has been talking a great deal,' he said.

Megan blushed. ' She was telling me about all her family,' she explained.

' I see,' he said shortly.

' Anyway,' Megan said crossly, ' I don't see why you should mind my knowing how old you are. You know how old I am!'

He smiled slowly. ' I don't mind your knowing that!'

' Then what did you mind?' she prompted him.

She thought he wasn't going to answer, but in the

end he did. 'They always had each other. I was too old to play with them, and their mother wasn't my mother. I expect I resented always being the odd man out.'

'But you are the eldest son!' Megan pointed out. 'You were always that!' She hesitated. 'I expect it's that that's made you so interfering,' she added impertinently. 'Rescuing strange females——'

'*That* had nothing to do with my responsibilities as the eldest son!' he cut in sharply.

'Of course it did!' retorted Megan, well pleased with her theory. 'I was just another Pilar, or Isabel, to you! I could feel it!'

'Indeed?' he said stiffly.

'Well, what other reason had you?' Megan asked reasonably.

'I suppose that one will do as well as any other,' he said with a glint of humour.

Megan's eyes widened. 'But it *must* have been your reason!'

He bowed slightly. 'If you say so.'

She chewed on her lip thoughtfully, wanting to puncture his confidence—just once—with the same ease with which he undermined hers. It wasn't only that he had the advantage in years and experience, for she had always before been able to give as good as she got, no matter who; it was more that he intimidated her *physically*, without even touching her, because for some peculiar reason she felt weak at the knees at the sight of him.

'I expect lunch will be ready soon,' she said finally. 'I'd better go and set the table.' She jumped up out of her chair and left the room in a rush, almost colliding with Pilar in the hall.

Pilar's eyes danced with anticipation. 'Did he ask you? Are you going to Mallorca?' She looked at Megan's face more closely. 'Did he upset you?' she demanded at last, her eye kindling.

'No, of course not! And yes, I am going to Majorca—'

'Ah!' Pilar grinned happily. 'I am so glad! If you hadn't, you know, I should have had to leave Barcelona, and that wouldn't have suited me at all!'

'No?'

Pilar looked wicked. 'There is a certain man I know—'

'Do I know him?' her brother's voice cut across their conversation.

Pilar's face fell. 'I have never seen him alone,' she said quickly. 'You know his sister!' she added. 'So perhaps you do know him!'

Carlos eyed her coldly. 'We'll talk about it later,' he said quietly. 'Now we had better join the others.'

Lunch was a painful meal as far as Megan was concerned. Her parents looked smug, as if they had pulled off a successful deal against incredible odds, and Pilar was still sulking in case her brother prevented her from seeing her friend in Barcelona ever again, though how he could do such a thing was quite beyond Megan.

It was a relief to her when the meal came to an end and she made her escape into the kitchen to make the coffee.

'May I carry the tray for you?' Carlos asked her.

'Thank you, but I can manage, *señor*,' she said with dignity.

He didn't offer again. Instead he stood and watched her as she made the coffee and placed the cups and saucers on a tray, together with a jug of cream and a bowl of brown sugar. When she had done, she picked up the tray and started off for the sitting room where the others were waiting, but somehow the kitchen door began to close just as she was walking through it, catching the edge of the tray, and some of the hot coffee spilled over on to her fingers.

Carlos snatched the tray from her and put it down

on the table. Megan put her scalded fingers behind her back, swallowing down unbidden tears, and wishing that he wouldn't look at her.

He turned on the cold tap and pulled her over to the sink, forcing her hands under the flow of water.

'That'll take the sting out,' he said cheerfully. He touched the pink patches that the hot coffee had made with incredible gentleness. 'There! You won't feel it in a few minutes.'

'It was all your fault!' she wailed.

'*Naturalmente lo dice en broma,*' he drawled.

'I don't understand Spanish,' she said sourly.

'I said you must be joking!'

'Well, it was your fault! Why couldn't you stay with the others?'

'I preferred to be with you,' he said.

'Nonsense!' she rebuked him with some asperity.

'May I carry the tray this time?' he suggested, unabashed.

She knew that she was being silly, but she couldn't help it. 'I'm not helpless!' she exclaimed.

His eyebrows rose. 'I didn't suppose that you were. A little spoilt, perhaps, but helpless? No!'

Megan looked at him. How could he say she was spoilt?

'I—I—' she began.

'It is more feminine to accept an offer of this sort graciously,' he said, with a remarkable lack of interest in her as a person. 'A Spanish woman learns that sort of thing in her pram!'

'Oh, really?' she said coldly.

He grinned at her. 'But it's not too late for you. You're young yet!' he taunted her. He picked up the tray and strode out of the kitchen and across the hall into the sitting room. Megan could hear her mother telling him how kind it was of him to bother and could have wept. Why was it that all the doors had behaved perfectly for him? Life was extremely unfair!

The afternoon was endless. Pilar and Carlos showed every sign that they were enjoying themselves. Mr Meredith stoked up the fire in the sitting room and had them toasting crumpets in front of its warmth, while Mrs Meredith pretended to do some mending and fussed over Megan, her mind jumping from one article to another of the things she thought Megan ought to take with her to Majorca.

'I've got all tomorrow to think about that,' Megan told her, exasperated.

'But Mrs Vallori will want you to look nice—'

'Don't I always?' Megan asked her dryly.

'In your own way,' her mother admitted. 'But I hope you'll be *tidier*, dear, when you're there!' She emitted a sigh of satisfaction. 'It's so nice to have no further worries about you! You're so thin, darling. I'm sure you haven't been eating properly in London by yourself.'

'It's fashionable to be thin!' Megan protested. 'Isn't it, Pilar?'

The Spanish girl nodded her head, smiling. 'But even I think you are thin, Megan. That dress is too wide for you—'

'The word is slim!' Megan interrupted her, crosser than ever.

Carlos chuckled. 'A yard of pump-water,' he teased her.

'If you're going to be *horrid*—' Megan flared at him.

'No, no,' he denied hastily. 'It is just an expression I heard somewhere. I find you very pleasant to look at.'

For some reason this didn't please Megan either. 'It's very bad manners to make personal remarks!' she said loftily.

His dark eyes lit with laughter. 'But not to children!' he excused himself.

'I'm not a child!'

'Of course you are still a child,' her mother put in

placidly.

Megan glared at her. 'At least I have the law on my side!' she muttered.

Pilar put a comforting hand on her shoulder. 'Carlos is always like that!' she pouted at her brother. 'But you will have the last word! Do you know what *dragonear* means? It is the Mallorquin word for courting a young lady at her window. You will have more suitors than Mama will be able to deal with. Then let them say that you are a child!'

Carlos laughed out loud. 'Then we'll call her a minx!'

Pilar looked at him coldly. 'You are not above courting the ladies yourself,' she reminded him. 'I know!'

'I am a man of valour!' Carlos drawled. 'I put my hand in the dragon's mouth and come away unscathed.'

Pilar giggled, unable to keep up her disapproval of anyone for very long.

'Tell them the story, Carlos! Tell them! It will amuse Megan to hear that Mallorca has its own St George!'

'It is a true story,' he began. 'You can see the proof in the Diocesan Museum behind the Cathedral in Palma, if you don't believe me. It was a long time ago now, perhaps about the year 1700, and Palma was in a state of terror because this dragon was living there. It preyed upon anyone who went out at night, and on anyone whose faith was weak, and sometimes it was seen prowling beneath the gratings in the street. Once, it nearly carried off a young boy, and the whole city was in a state of panic. Nobody dared to go out at all after dark, and a reward was offered for the dragon's capture, but nobody was brave enough to engage the dread beast. The Governor of Alcudia, a young man called Don Bernardo Coch, used to go to visit his fiancée in Palma just the same. He used to ride

41

into Palma on a very fine horse and make love to his beloved through the window. But one night the dragon appeared, breathing fire through its nostrils. The girl was badly frightened, but Don Bernardo was quite pleased to be able to prove his courage to his sweetheart. He drew his sword and attacked the dragon, killing it dead!'

'It's absolutely true!' Pilar exclaimed, seeing Megan's ironic expression. 'The Mallorquins were terribly grateful to Don Bernardo. They called the dragon after his betrothed, *El Drac de Na Coca*! There used to be a festival every year when the dragon was shown to the people! It was kept by the Roselló Miralles family, the descendants of Don Bernardo, and they gave it to the museum!'

'I don't believe it!' Megan said flatly.

Carlos looked amused. 'You can see for yourself when you are in Palma,' he said.

'But,' Megan said reasonably, 'nobody courts people through a window nowadays!'

'Don't you find it romantic?' Pilar asked anxiously. 'I should love someone to sing songs to me outside my window!' She caught her brother's eye and coloured a little. 'Someone I—like,' she ended lamely.

Megan rubbed her nose with her forefinger. 'I should find it embarrassing,' she said gruffly.

'That is because you are not in love,' Carlos told her.

'I'd feel a fool!'

'He'd be a brave man!' Carlos said thoughtfully.

Megan's defences dropped from her. 'Why?' she demanded, sounding as hurt as she felt. 'I suppose you think I'd sing right back at him? Stealing his thunder?'

He looked surprised. 'No, that hadn't occurred to me. I was thinking of the scorching you'd give him for not daring to speak to you face to face. A dragon indeed!'

She blushed. ' I'm not as unromantic as you think!' she protested.

' No?'

Her eyes fell before the teasing look in his. ' No,' she said. ' I have my moments like everyone else!'

' Is that a promise?' he drawled.

Megan pretended she hadn't heard him. She jumped to her feet and looked out at the white, winter scene and the grey sky that threatened yet more snow. ' It's going to snow again,' she said.

' Then we had better be going,' he said amiably. ' I will return for you here on Tuesday?'

She shook her head. ' I'll meet you in London,' she told him.

She thought he was going to argue with her, but he only nodded in a businesslike way. ' Very well. What's your address?'

She wrote it down for him, together with the telephone number. He accepted the slip of paper, putting it carefully away in his leather wallet.

' You will not fail me?' he said finally, as he eased himself into his coat.

Megan shook her head. ' I'll—I'll try to make your mother happier,' she promised earnestly. ' But I haven't much experience—'

He laid a finger on her cheek. ' Be happy yourself, that's all that's needed!'

She sniffed. ' That's easy!' she scoffed.

He looked down at her for a long moment. ' I hope so,' he said at last. ' I wonder if I'm wise to let you loose in the dragon's cave?'

She wrinkled up her nose, not sure that she knew what he meant. ' I can look after myself!' she assured him.

' Without getting your fingers burned?'

' That was an accident! *Dragons* don't frighten me!'

' If you recognise them in time!'

43

She chuckled. 'Are you sure you're not talking about wolves?' she asked him demurely.

He shrugged his shoulders. 'You have wolves in your cold climate, we have fiery breathed dragons in the sun!' He laughed suddenly. 'They say you must fight fire with fire, but I think you are too young, *amada*, for us to find out, no?'

Megan put her hands behind her back like a child. 'I don't know what you mean,' she said.

'Obviously not,' he said on a sigh. 'I'll see you on Tuesday?'

She nodded, relieved that they were going. She went with them to the car and waved to them as they disappeared down the drive, Pilar's scarlet coat showing up as a bright splash of colour in the black and white scene. She was glad they had gone, but she felt inexpressibly lonely at their going.

On the telephone, Carlos's Spanish accent was clearly discernible. He sounded foreign and more alien than she had remembered him. She thought, with a feeling of rising panic, that she didn't understand him at all, and that she probably wouldn't even like his mother! She was mad to be going to Majorca at all! She should have stayed exactly where she was and got on with her career by finding another singing engagement somewhere. Jobs didn't grow on trees, of course, but she would have found *something*, sooner or later.

'Megan? I have booked you to fly to Mallorca at nine o'clock tomorrow morning. I will be at your address at seven. That will give us time to get to the airport before eight. You will be ready?'

'Yes,' Megan said simply.

There was a short pause at the other end. 'I shall be travelling to Mallorca with you,' his voice came again, sounding unexpectedly diffident.

'I thought you were going to Barcelona!'

'I was,' he said flatly. 'My stepmother wishes me

to help her open up the house in Palma, however.'

'But can't I do that?' Megan suggested, a little overcome that he should change his plans at his stepmother's whim.

'My stepmother requires someone who can speak Spanish to be with her for a few days,' he explained. 'Apparently she is planning to change the decorations and to put in an extra bathroom. She wishes me to deal with the workmen for her.'

'Oh, I see,' Megan said inadequately.

'I thought you might be pleased?'

She was glad that he couldn't see her face, for she could feel herself blushing.

'I am!' she said.

'Good. That is better than I hoped!'

'Oh?' She sounded shocked and rather pleased.

'Tomorrow you must tell me exactly how pleased you are,' he continued, his voice edged with laughter.

'Oh!' she said again.

'*Hasta luego*, Megan Meredith.'

Megan giggled, sufficiently encouraged to try out her own Spanish. '*Hasta la vista, señor*,' she said demurely, and replaced the receiver quickly before he had a chance to make any further remark.

She stood for a long moment, looking into space, trying to still her whirring thoughts. Then she put on her coat and hurried out before the shops closed to buy a Spanish grammar and a phrase book to help her over those first awkward days. If she applied herself, she thought, she might be able to say something more to Señor Carlos Vallori Llobera in his own language. She could imagine his dark green eyes crinkling with pleased surprise and the thought warmed her as she hurried down the street. In a few weeks she would be able to say anything, anything at all!

Megan felt heavy-eyed after an almost sleepless night. She carried her suitcase down the numerous flights of stairs that led up to the room she shared with her ex-school friend and dropped it with a bang on to the lino-covered floor of the main hall. When she opened the front door, she saw that it was snowing again.

'We are both a little early,' Carlos greeted her, doffing his hat to her. 'Is your luggage upstairs? Shall I fetch it?'

'It's here,' she said awkwardly. She lifted the heavy suitcase and shoved it through the doorway, slamming the front door behind her. 'I hope it isn't overweight. I seem to have packed just about everything I possess!'

Carlos looked down at the suitcase. 'In that?' he asked.

'It's my father's case really,' she confessed. 'It's the largest one we have.'

He took it from her, carrying it with the greatest of ease, and put it in the back of the car.

'Is that really all you possess in the world?' he asked her, as he held the door for her to get in.

She nodded shyly, very conscious of his long length standing so close to her.

'I suppose you have not had long to collect much clutter from living,' he teased her. 'I cannot remember a time when all I possess would have fitted into one suitcase!'

'That's different,' she said.

'Is it?' He slammed her door shut and went round to the driving seat, jumping in beside her and turning on the ignition key in the one easy movement.

'I don't own any houses, or furniture, or anything like that,' Megan said simply. She smiled suddenly. '*I'm* not the eldest son of a Spanish family!'

'I'm glad you're not!' he said gravely.

'I don't know——' she began, then stopped. 'You mean, you're glad I'm not a boy—that I'm a girl?' She stopped again, looking resolutely out of the window at the falling snow. 'I mean, I'm an only child,' she said.

'I meant that I am glad you are a girl, *pequeña*,'

46

he agreed, smiling.

Megan was silent, savouring the moment. The car started forward, the tyres slipping a little on the crushed snow.

'Do you think any planes will be taking off in this?' she asked him.

'Will you mind waiting, Meganita, if we have to?'

The endearment added to her name pleased her. 'N-no,' she said uncertainly. 'I find airports rather exciting places. I like to hear the names of all the different places being called out.'

But in the end their plane was not held up. The snow had been brushed off the wings and the snow-ploughs had been busy all along the length of the airstrip. The Comet IV heaved itself into the air and climbed up above the snow clouds and into the pale, wintry sunshine.

'All right, *amada*?'

Megan nodded eagerly. 'What will the weather be like when we land?' she asked him.

'It will be sunny, with the temperature about fifteen degrees. That will take the shadows away from under your eyes!'

'I haven't got any!' she denied. 'Fifteen,' she mused. 'That's about sixty, isn't it?'

He shrugged his shoulders, producing a whole lot of papers out of his briefcase. 'Have you something to read?' he asked meaningly.

She smiled and produced a paperback out of her handbag, but she had no intention of reading anything so dull as the thriller she had with her. Instead, she watched, fascinated, as the stewardesses hurried up and down the aisle, selling their tax-free wares, serving breakfast to the passengers and tending to their needs, as the plane raced onwards towards warmer climes.

After a while, Megan felt sleepy and she sat well back in her seat, finding that she could study Carlos' profile without even moving her head. She found she

47

liked looking at him. His clean, tanned skin pleased her as much as she liked the green of his eyes and the tough springiness of his black hair. Then, quite suddenly, he felt her eyes on him and he looked up enquiringly. She was hotly embarrassed and returned quickly to her neglected book. Without a word, he stretched out a hand and took it from her, stuffing it into the pocket in the rear of the seat in front of her.

'Your breakfast,' he told her.

She accepted the cardboard tray from the stewardess, suddenly aware that she was hungry, and broke into the plastic cover eagerly. The rolls were fresh and crisp and she spread them with butter and jam, eating them quickly while she waited for another stewardess to bring their coffee.

'I didn't eat much last night,' she explained, wriggling a little under Carlos' amused gaze.

'It doesn't look as though you slept much either,' he said frankly. 'What were you doing? Packing? Or painting the town red one last time?'

She winced. 'The girl-friend I share with was away,' she said flatly. 'I didn't do anything in particular.'

'I thought your mother might come up for the night and to see you off this morning?' he said curiously.

Megan shook her head. 'She would never leave my father.'

He looked at her curiously. 'Are you often alone?' he asked.

She made an attempt to laugh off his enquiry, but in the end she couldn't. 'It works both ways,' she said at last. 'I can't imagine myself cancelling all my arrangements because my mother wanted to put in an extra bathroom either!'

'But that is family life!' he exclaimed.

'In Spain,' she said. 'In England it's different.'

'Perhaps,' he said, but she could tell that he didn't believe her. She smarted a little under his implied

48

criticism of her own family and longed to defend them, though quite what from she didn't know.

'In the last resort they'd do anything for me!' she declared.

'I am sure they would,' he smiled. 'But one does not live continually in the last resort!'

That struck her as funny and she laughed. 'Speak for yourself!' she admonished him. 'I'm not sure that I don't!'

He smiled and collected up their empty breakfast trays, pointing out of the window to the grey mountains beneath them. 'Mallorca!'

With mounting excitement, Megan stared down at the island below her. It was considerably bigger than she had thought, and it was hard to see much of what it was really like, for the clouds drifted beneath them, hiding the land from her eager eyes. Then, unexpectedly, the sun broke through the clouds and she was able to see literally hundreds of windmills beneath them.

A few minutes later, Palma appeared, together with the long, sandy beach, edged from end to end with hotels. The engine note changed and there was a faint bump as they landed. Just two hours and twenty minutes after leaving England, they had arrived in Majorca.

CHAPTER IV

Señora Vallori was waiting for them outside the airport in the car. Carlos hurried their suitcases through the Customs and then led Megan out into the sunlight. He kissed his stepmother on the cheek and introduced Megan to her, leaving them to get into the car while he stowed the luggage away in the boot.

'Have you known Carlos long, Miss Meredith?' Señora Vallori asked her.

Megan shook her head. 'I don't know him well,' she admitted.

'But you like him?'

'I like both him and Pilar,' Megan answered carefully. 'They both came to lunch with my parents.'

'Pilar is *my* daughter,' Señora Vallori said with pride. 'She is devoted to Carlos—always has been. He takes her about with him quite often. Isabel, my other daughter, is more reserved. You haven't met her?'

'No,' Megan agreed.

Señora Vallori sank back into the car with a sigh of relief. Looking at her, Megan could hardly believe that she was English. To begin with, she was the only person she had ever seen who wore the traditional Spanish comb in her hair, complete with mantilla, which she used to veil the sides of her face. She was not particularly tall, but she looked shorter than she was, for she was more than a little plump and her legs were shorter than is usual in an Englishwoman.

'Do you mind sitting in the back?' she asked Megan indolently. 'We only have this little Seat in Mallorca —not at all comfortable!—but they are excellent for the narrow streets in Palma, and just adequate for the rest of the island.'

'I don't mind at all,' Megan assured her. She

pushed the driving seat forward and struggled into the back, watched lazily by her hostess who made not the slightest effort to help her. 'You have two houses here, don't you? I expect you have a lot to do, running both of them and the almond orchard too?'

The Señora laughed in the back of her throat. 'Not I! My husband spoilt me dreadfully when he was alive and I never had to stir hand or foot. Carlos doesn't approve of the result, but he realises it's too late to change me now!' She said this with such satisfaction that Megan was faintly shocked, but she said nothing. Carlos folded his long length into the driver's seat and turned on the ignition key, nosing the car away from the kerb and away from the airport.

'Well, how are things, Margot?' he asked his stepmother lazily.

'I have been in flat despair,' the Señora answered placidly. 'I can't think why you suppose it's a good idea for me to live here, *caro*. It's only February, but the whole place is swarming with tourists! What will it be like in the summer?'

'You'll shut yourself inside behind the shutters whatever it's like,' he retorted callously, 'so I can't see that they need bother you much!'

'If your father could hear you—'

'Come on now, Margot, you know it was his idea that you should live here!'

'Was it?' The Señora smiled bravely. 'Perhaps it won't be as bad as I think, but I should have liked to have gone to England.'

'It isn't as you remember it,' he told her flatly. 'Ask Megan!'

The Señora stirred herself to look over her shoulder at Megan. 'Carlos will have it that London has changed in the last few years, but I don't believe him. London has always had a quality of its own!'

Megan wasn't sure whether she was being asked her opinion or not. 'I like London too,' she admitted.

'There you are!' the Señora said complacently. 'Megan agrees with me!'

'Megan would hardly remember the London you are talking about,' her stepson said dryly. 'She's just a baby!'

'She looks fully grown to me,' the Señora drawled.

Megan felt herself blushing, but she was grateful that *somebody* thought she was old enough to have an opinion.

'Do you think so?' Carlos laughed.

'She's a bit thin,' the Señora went on, 'but that's better than the other way about. How old are you, Megan?'

'She's eighteen,' Carlos answered for her.

'Old enough!' the Señora grunted enigmatically.

Carlos grinned at his stepmother. 'Don't get ideas, Margot!'

The older woman chuckled comfortably. 'I won't, if you don't! How is Pilar?'

Megan shut her ears to the family chat going on in front of her and stared out at the strange sights all about her. The windmills were almost all stationary, and some of them looked to be in bad repair, but there were so many of them, drawing up the water to irrigate the land, that they dominated the area, only losing their importance when they slipped on to the motorway that led straight into Palma.

The little car sped along the highway, slowing only as they came into the city just below the Cathedral. Carlos drove fast and well, even when the traffic grew thicker, turning this way and that without apparently giving any warning at all of their intentions. At the major crossroads, a traffic policeman was stationed on a high red and white stand, blowing his whistle frantically whenever some intrepid driver ignored his instructions; at other junctions there were traffic lights, the red light twice the size of the green and amber, but even so rather difficult to see.

Then, in hardly any time at all, Carlos turned off into the Plaza Santa Eulalia and down the narrow Calle Morey. He drew up in front of the heavy wooden doors of one of the houses, that were left open to reveal the patio inside, around which the house was built. Megan leaned forward eagerly, delighted by the patterned marble tiles that covered the floor, the flowering plants that had been placed about the playing fountain, the elegant steps that led up into the house itself, half hidden behind the upstairs terrace that rested on fluted columns taking the eye upwards from the patio below.

'It's beautiful!' she breathed.

'Do you think so?' the Señora asked, surprised. 'I'm not very keen on the Italian influence myself. It looks nice enough, but it doesn't make for comfort!'

'I'd put up with quite a lot of discomfort to have a patio and a staircase like that!' Megan exclaimed.

The Señora looked amused. 'You must ask Carlos to tell you the history of the house. If you like it, the inside is a gem of its kind too. I don't like it.'

'I don't see how you could help it!'

The Señora smiled. 'You're younger than I thought,' she remarked. 'Age brings a desire for comfort, and there's very little of that in this house!'

'Still complaining?' Carlos asked his stepmother cheerfully as he pushed the suitcases through the open doors into the patio. 'Take Megan inside, will you, Margot? I'll get rid of the car.'

The Señora stood beside the fountain, eyeing the suitcases with distaste. 'What a lot of luggage you have!' she exclaimed.

Megan felt uncomfortable. 'Only one suitcase is mine,' she defended herself. 'The other two belong to Carlos.'

The Señora's face brightened. 'It looks as though he means to stay a little while this time. You've no idea how lonely it is when I am all by myself!'

Megan was just about to say something comforting when she was interrupted by the arrival of two maids who came scurrying out of the house, scolding the Señora for not calling them immediately. They grasped the suitcases and hurried up the wide staircase, chattering to each other as they went.

'We'd better go inside too,' the Señora said reluctantly. 'Don't worry about your things. Juana will unpack your clothes. She speaks a little English, by the way. She worked in one of the hotels until recently, but she prefers to be in a proper home and I pay excellent wages.'

Megan followed her up the stairs, pausing at intervals to admire the carved intricacies of the stone banisters. At the top was a long picture gallery, full of sombre paintings of the various Vallori ancestors. Megan would have liked to have studied them more closely, but the shutters kept out any light that might have crept into the house, and all she could see was the occasional pale, aristocratic face amongst the shadows.

The gallery led directly into a lofty salon, hung about with Flemish tapestries and full of Renaissance nailed seats, and a few chairs upholstered in leather. Megan was forced to agree that comfort had been sacrificed to the strict formality of the furnishings. It was hard to imagine anyone actually sitting in such a room, let alone relaxing.

'Do you use this room much?' she asked nervously.

The Señora screwed up her nose in horror. 'Never!'

Megan was relieved. It was beautiful of course, there was no denying that, but she couldn't feel at home there.

'We sit here,' the Señora went on, sweeping Megan into the next room. 'Once you've got used to the red pine panelling and the draughts that haunt the marble floors, and the total lack of any proper heating, it's just tolerable.'

Megan tried not to look as though she were too curious, but this room too was quite unlike any other sitting room she had ever seen. The few chairs were arranged in straight lines, facing each other, and there was a curious bronze contraption in the middle of the floor, held by a wooden frame, that had no possible use that she could see.

'When it's cold, we put a fire in that,' the Señora explained, her amusement getting the better of her apathy. 'It smokes rather, and it gives out remarkably little heat, but we're seldom here in the winter, so we never put in central heating like most of our neighbours.' She thrust open a shutter, allowing a shaft of light into the darkened room. 'Can you understand why I don't want to be banished here?'

'Yes,' Megan said flatly.

The dark eyes of the older woman met hers, a twinkle lurking in their depths. 'I thought you would fall in love with the place?' she said.

'I have!' Megan agreed. 'But it is cold, and it is a little like a museum. Couldn't we make it a little more comfortable, *señora*? Then it would be a truly lovely place to live!'

'It would be such a lot of trouble,' the Señora objected.

'Not really!' Megan's quick enthusiasm was now thoroughly aroused. 'You could have an English style room for your own use! Think how much more comfortable you would be then!'

The Señora shrugged. 'You can suggest it to Carlos if you like,' she said with apparent indifference. 'He wouldn't like it if I were to suggest such a thing! He's never liked changes in anything connected with his family.'

'But that's ridiculous!' Megan exclaimed. 'Most of the house would be just as it was! Besides, one can't live entirely in the past, no matter how beautiful! I'm sure your son will see that!'

'My stepson,' the Señora corrected her automatically.

'It makes no difference!' Megan said warmly.

'What makes no difference?' Carlos asked from the doorway. He looked very much at home in the rich, formal room. He might even, Megan thought, sit upright in the uncomfortable chairs and think nothing of it. He shared the same elegance, the same richness as the ancient house.

'Megan wishes to make this room more habitable,' his stepmother drawled. 'She agrees with me that it is not very comfortable as it is.'

Carlos looked about him in surprise. 'What's wrong with it?' he demanded.

For an instant Megan thought he was angry, but the lift of his eyebrows reassured her. 'It doesn't look as though anyone ever sat in here in their lives,' she told him frankly. 'It's—it's like a museum!'

'I suppose it is,' he agreed, looking amused. 'It is certainly very different from your parents' house! But I am not sure that you can make this room look the same as theirs?'

'I wouldn't try!' she exclaimed. 'My parents' room is *comfortable*, but it isn't—' She broke off, blushing uncontrollably.

'You wouldn't choose it?' the Señora put in helpfully.

'N-no,' Megan agreed quickly. 'It isn't *elegant*.'

Carlos gave her an interested look. 'I agree with you. It is warm and comfortable, but there are pieces of furniture that I should not care to live with myself.' He hesitated. 'Very well, Megan, I give you a free hand to do what you will with this room. But the rest of the house shall be kept as it is for the time being.'

'But your stepmother—'

Carlos stiffened. 'Margot cannot be bothered with domestic matters,' he said tersely.

The Señora shrugged her shoulders. 'Why should

I?' she said. 'I prefer that other people should do these things for me.'

Megan looked from one to the other of them. 'I'll do my best,' she promised. 'But it might cost a bit of money.'

'Undoubtedly,' Carlos agreed dryly. 'English type furniture is expensive anywhere but in England.'

'And you don't mind?' Megan pressed him.

'Not if the results are satisfactory,' he confirmed. 'Have you seen your room?' He waited for her to shake her head. 'I suppose Juana is unpacking for you. Meanwhile, you may as well see the rest of the house.'

He took her consent for granted, pushing open the door at the far end of the salon. 'In the old days,' he told her, 'when we held dances here, we would open all the doors and make use of the whole floor. But that was a long time ago. These doors have become stiff with lack of use since then.'

'It would make a magnificent setting for a dance,' Megan said dreamily.

'You like it?' Somehow the question seemed important to him and she considered it carefully before answering.

'Yes,' she said at last, 'I love it!'

'You love easily!' he taunted her.

Megan stepped through the open door ahead of him, embarrassed. He had a knack of making her feel gauche and peculiarly naïve.

'I don't think I do,' she said seriously. 'I like easily—but loving is a different matter!'

'So it is!' he agreed laconically.

The room was so dark that she could only make out dim shapes that she took to be bookcases. Carlos opened the shutters and turned to face her.

'This is my particular sanctuary. The rest of the family doesn't often come in here.'

And never without his permission, Megan thought

57

wryly. She was surprised, though, at his choice of room to make his own. This had originally been the library, and books still lined the walls, but it was now a study-cum-workroom, with a huge, elaborate desk at one end, a couple of easy chairs placed negligently before the carved stone fireplace, and a huge heraldic emblem covering the far wall, as aggressively arrogant as Megan felt Carlos to be himself.

'The Vaylori arms?' she asked, keeping her voice as blank as possible.

'No. Those are the Llobera arms. My mother was the only child of her generation and the last of the

'The Valori arms?' she asked, keeping her voice family.'

Megan felt unaccountably sad. 'Aren't there any of them left?'

'I have my grandmother still alive, and an unmarried aunt. That's all.'

'But there are lots of Valloris?'

Carlos smiled. 'More than enough,' he agreed. 'At one time my father used to hang his own arms and my mother's side by side in our house in Barcelona, but when he married again, Margot objected that her predecessor's presence in the house was greater than her own, so my father took down my mother's arms and put them away. I came across them by chance and brought them here. I am very proud to have them.'

Megan's eyes filled with tears. 'You must have been hurt,' she said bluntly.

He shrugged, 'Small boys are always imagining woes for themselves!'

'Well, I think it was mean!' Megan insisted.

He laughed at her. 'Would you have allowed them to stay?' he asked ironically.

She nodded her head defiantly. 'Yes, I would! I'd have been proud of them!'

His mouth curled in disbelief. 'I think not.'

'But I would! They wouldn't only be a reminder

that my husband had been married before, they would have been a part of *you*!' She stopped, a little shocked by what she had said. 'I mean, you'd have been there anyway,' she went on uncomfortably.

'Another constant reminder!'

Megan's eyes widened. 'But one couldn't be jealous of a small boy!' she exclaimed.

He looked at her closely. 'Perhaps you would not be,' he conceded, catching a tear on his forefinger as it brimmed over her eyelashes. 'It is hard to know that the son and heir is already waiting to inherit when you have your own children to consider, though. Pepe has always had to come second to me, except in his mother's affections.'

Megan backed away from him, ashamed that he should have seen her tears. 'I would have tried to love you equally with my own children,' she said obstinately.

'Perhaps Margot *tried* too!'

'I don't see how she could have helped it! You can't have been very old—'

'Old enough to be difficult. I refused to speak a word of English to her for a long time. The Spanish are a proud people, and I have all the pride of my race. I am sure I was a thorn in her flesh, as I meant to be. Not at all the forsaken small boy that a woman could have loved!'

'*I* would have loved you!'

'Would you?' he asked very gently.

She nodded fiercely. 'You wouldn't have got the better of me!' she declared. 'I'd think pretty poorly of myself if I couldn't win the affection of one small boy, Spanish or not!'

Carlos looked amused. 'I think you probably would have succeeded,' he admitted. 'It would have been a novel experience to have had a pretty girl crying over me!'

'I'm *not* crying!' she said crossly.

'No?' His eyes mocked her. 'You're very young, Megan.'

She glared at him. 'What's that got to do with it?'

'More than you think,' he retorted. 'If you were older you wouldn't break your heart over a boy who doesn't exist any more!'

Megan bit her lip. 'I think he does,' she said in a whisper.

'In me?'

She nodded briefly. 'What is the rest of the house like?' she asked quickly.

He put his hands on her shoulders and turned her to face the light, whether she would or no. 'There is very little of the small boy left in me,' he told her grimly. 'I grew up a long time ago!'

'Oh?' She forced herself to sound light and amused, but she felt neither.

'Do you doubt it?'

She licked her lips nervously. 'No,' she said.

His hands tightened on her shoulders, pulling her against him. She turned her head away, afraid that he meant to kiss her, and even more afraid of her own possible reaction.

'I—I'd like to go to my room!'

'It is you who hasn't grown up,' he chided her impatiently.

She freed herself impatiently from his restraining hands. 'I'm old enough to prefer to be taken seriously!' she informed him loftily. 'More than old enough!'

'Seriously?' he repeated.

'As a woman!' she added self-consciously. She couldn't help feeling that she was destroying her own case by having to point it out to him.

'Indeed?'

She saw the glint in his eyes and was afraid. This time there was no escaping the pressure of his hands. He held her tightly against him and kissed her hard on the mouth, parting her lips beneath his.

She had expected to dislike it, but it wasn't like that at all. It was the most exciting, the most marvellous experience of her whole life. She put her arms around his neck and hugged him closer still, wondering that any man should be able to stir her in this way. His hands moved down her back with an intimacy that alarmed even while it thrilled her. Then, as suddenly, she was free and he stood away from her, looking down at her as though she were a complete stranger to him.

' You see,' he said, ' you are too young to tell when a man is serious!'

She threw back her head, her expression as proud as his. ' You flatter yourself, *señor*. I know you would never be serious with a nobody like myself! Nor would I ever be serious over anyone as arrogant and selfish as yourself!'

' I told you the boy in me is dead,' he said coldly.

Her hands were shaking, so she put them behind her back to hide them from him.

' He isn't dead, *señor*. If he doesn't live on in the man you are now, it's because you deliberately destroyed him. I may be young, I may be *very* young, but I hope I never feel ashamed of what I was before—'

If she had hoped to anger, she had certainly succeeded. ' That is enough, Megan,' he snapped. ' You don't know what you are talking about.'

She was silent. She thought resentfully that it was easy enough for him to intimidate her at every turn and wished desperately that, just once, she might have the pleasure of placing him at a disadvantage. She pushed her hair back behind her ears and sniffed.

' Are you going to cry again?' he asked in exasperated tones.

' No.'

He stood quite still, waiting for her to recover her poise. ' Do you wish me to apologise?' he asked at last.

61

'No,' she said again.

'I think I should all the same,' he went on, not without humour. 'I fancy that no one has kissed you quite like that before—'

'Then you fancy wrong!' she answered proudly. 'I've been kissed *often* by heaps of people—'

'That is not precisely what I meant,' he interrupted dryly.

She cast him a startled glance, dismayed by the harshness of his expression and the unyielding look in his eyes.

'Then what did you mean?'

'I meant that you are very sweet and very innocent, no more than that—'

'And *boring*?'

'I didn't say that!' he replied, trying not to laugh.

'Well, I think innocence is boring,' she retorted unthinkingly.

'Perhaps that is where men and women differ in their approach to each other,' he suggested mildly.

She felt herself blushing. 'Then—then—'

'Then what?'

'You didn't *dislike* kissing me?'

He smiled at her anxious expression. 'No,' he said, 'I didn't dislike it.'

She breathed a sigh of relief. He seemed to be waiting for something, though, and she supposed that he was hoping to hear what she had thought of the kiss, just as she had wanted to know about his reaction.

'I didn't dislike it either,' she said abruptly.

He reached for her hand and raised it to his lips, kissing her palm and curling her fingers inwards to hold the place he had touched.

'You are very generous,' he said. 'That was much more than I deserved.'

She almost ran to the doorway in her eagerness to escape from the challenge his very presence presented her with.

'I don't see why,' she said over her shoulder. 'You're probably very practised. Pilar says you know lots of women!'

'Pilar talks too much!'

'I suppose you think she shouldn't know about such things!' Megan added provocatively.

'Not necessarily. But, like you, I prefer not to be discussed behind my back!'

She was immediately contrite. 'We weren't really,' she assured him. 'We were talking about your step-mother wanting to live in England. Pilar said that everyone expected you to marry very well and that they had expected the same of your father, only he fell in love with your stepmother and that was that!'

'They were very much in love,' Carlos confirmed unexpectedly.

'And you?' Megan asked before she could stop herself.

'Me? Will I marry well?'

'Will you marry for love?'

His dark eyes were enigmatic and very arrogant as he looked at her. 'I hardly think that is any business of yours,' he said tersely.

'No,' she agreed, feeling snubbed.

'The woman I have chosen to be my wife will be very much loved,' he went on smoothly. 'She will be important because she will be my wife and the mother of my children. Does that answer you?'

Megan's spirits sank and she knew a sudden envy of this unknown woman who was going to be Carlos' wife.

'I suppose she's very lovely?' she heard herself say.

'I think so,' he answered calmly. 'One day you will be able to tell me what you think.'

'No!' she burst out passionately. 'I don't want to!'

His eyebrows rose enquiringly. Megan swallowed desperately, but the lump in her throat obstinately refused to be dislodged.

'Come,' he said gently, 'I will show you your room.

The rest of the house can wait for another time.'

He strode past her, opening and shutting doors with an unconcern that made her own nervousness of him seem all the more unnecessary. She was bitterly conscious of the way her heart thudded within her as she followed him meekly through the house and up the marble stairs to the bedrooms above.

'My stepmother's room is here,' he said as they gained the top of the stairs. 'Your room is opposite.' He opened the door with a flourish, his eyes mocking her. 'You should feel quite safe in here!'

Megan would have liked to have asked him where his room was, but she knew better than to give him such an opening. He wouldn't spare her feelings, she thought, if he ever guessed how easily he stirred her emotions and how certain little things about him caught at her heartstrings, leaving her more vulnerable than she had ever been before in all her eighteen years.

She stepped into the room and stopped. It was like nothing she had ever seen before. An enormous four-poster bed took up the whole of the centre of the room, heavy curtains draped about it and gathered up together in a kind of knotted effect just below the ceiling, itself surmounted by what looked suspiciously like a coronet. Beneath the window was an oak chest, heavily carved and very ancient. On the other side of the bed was a marble-topped dresser, complete with a patterned china bowl and jug for washing purposes. It was the grandest and most awful room she had ever seen.

'I'm to sleep here?' she gasped.

Carlos eyed the bed meaningly. 'Will it disturb your dreams?' he teased her.

'Of course not,' she denied hastily.

'It's more comfortable than it looks,' he told her kindly.

'Have you slept in it?' she demanded, prodding the mattress nervously. It was big enough for four people to sleep in, she thought. She had never seen such an enormous bed.

'Often,' Carlos said dryly. 'This was my room when I was a boy, in fact until quite recently when I moved into my father's old room. Perhaps that's why my stepmother chose it for you.' He smiled at her aghast expression and, turning on his heel, shut the door with a snap behind him, leaving her alone with her chaotic thoughts.

CHAPTER V

'You'd better call me Margot,' Señora Vallori suggested.

Megan nodded. 'If you want me to.'

'It makes me feel old to be addressed as Señora all the time. Heaven knows, it makes me feel old enough to have a companion wished on to me.'

Megan felt uncomfortable. She wriggled in her chair and looked at the sunshine outside, seeking inspiration from its warmth.

'I thought you wanted someone English to live with you here—that you were lonely—'

'So I am!'

'Oh,' Megan said inadequately, 'I suppose it isn't the same as going to England as you had wanted to.'

Señora Vallori sighed. 'Carlos tells me that England isn't the same as I remember it. I suppose he's right. I'm used to the comfort of living in Spain now. The Spaniards give their women such a lovely, *protected* feeling!'

Megan was on the point of arguing with her about that, but she changed her mind, reflecting that she was not married to a Spaniard, and was never likely to be, and that therefore what seemed like loving protection to her employer seemed like a whole lot of petty restrictions to herself.

'Can you drive a car?' the Señora asked suddenly.

Megan nodded eagerly. 'I drive my father's car sometimes. He gave me some driving lessons for my birthday. But isn't it more difficult having to drive on the right?'

'Makes no difference at all!' the Señora assured her. 'It's useful that you can drive, though. You can take yourself about the island and see the sights.'

Megan's eyes widened in protest. ' But I ought to be doing things for you—'

' So you shall, dear. Only I am not exactly in my dotage and so I don't need anyone to wait on me all the time.'

' In fact,' said Megan, ' you don't know what to do with a companion now you have one!'

Señora Vallori looked mildly embarrassed. ' You're very welcome! You must know that! I expect I shall find lots of things for you to do in a little while, my dear, but as we already have two maids and a gardener-cum-chauffeur, there doesn't seem to be a great deal for you to do at the moment.'

' I can't think why Carlos suggested my coming,' Megan said abruptly.

' Nor can I, dear, but I expect he had his reasons. And you are going to do up the small sitting-room, aren't you? Why don't you get on with that?'

Megan stood up. ' It's a little difficult to shop as I don't speak any Spanish yet. May I go and look round the shops? Perhaps I'll get some ideas that way.'

' Do,' the Señora invited her. ' By the time you get back Carlos may be in and you'll be able to talk to him.'

Megan gave her a startled glance. ' I don't think—' she began.

Señora Vallori's eyes hardened. ' Don't you?' She looked away again, the smile on her face never altering. ' Don't be late for dinner, dear, will you? We have guests coming.'

' No, I won't be late.' Megan gathered up her handbag in a sudden rush and hurried out of the room. She would go out, she decided. She would take her first look at Palma and try and feel a little less unwanted. It was so peculiar that Carlos should have brought her here if his stepmother didn't want or need an English companion. As for the Señora, she couldn't make up her mind about her. It was too early to know if she liked her. Most of what she had heard about her she didn't like at all. Megan repressed a faint shiver as she thought about her. All she really had against the Señora was that she wasn't a particularly kind person. She wasn't even thoughtlessly kind in the way that Megan's own mother was kind. She was charming and very sure of her own attractions, but she wasn't *kind*!

Megan passed down the magnificent steps into the patio, pausing for a moment to look at the potted flowers and some ornamental carvings that she hadn't noticed previously. A car zoomed past the entrance, taking up the whole of the narrow street, warning her to be cautious as she stepped outside and made her way towards the cathedral and the sea.

At the bottom of the street she wondered whether to turn left or right. Both looked equally unlikely. The streets were very old, narrow and shuttered, with the occasional line of washing hanging out of one of the secretive windows. Some women stood gossiping in the doorway of one of the houses, flattening themselves against the yellow ochre walls whenever a car crept along beside them. She turned left because a lorry was making a delivery in the street on the right. An old woman, dressed totally in black, eyed her curiously, turning right round in her carpet slippers to get a closer look, her toothless mouth hanging open in her astonishment.

It was soon obvious that she had gone the wrong way, but sooner than turn back she thought she would turn right and then right again as a pleasanter way of backtracking on the way she had come. The narrow street she chose was dark, lit only by the narrow slit of sky overhead, so Megan hurried down it as fast as she could, fearful of she knew not what.

Quite why the door caught her eye she didn't know, but there it was, painted in scarlet and green, with the legend *Baños Arabes* written round it. It was half

open, inviting her to peer through at the garden
beyond, at the brilliant colours of the anemones growing at least a foot high, at the geraniums and the
poinsettias, and other flowers that she couldn't put a
name to, and, best of all, the orange and the lemon
trees, full of fruit that was actually hanging on the
branches.

Megan took a step up into the garden and was
beckoned inside by an old man sitting on a wooden
form with his back to the wall.

' I'm so sorry,' she said in English. ' I was admiring
your garden.'

He smiled at her, leaping to his feet and holding
out his hand to her, apparently pleading with her to
come inside. ' *Buenas tardes, señorita!* '

' *Buenas tardes,*' she repeated shyly.

He gave her an encouraging look and stamped off
down the path, beckoning her to follow him. She did
so, not liking to seem ungracious when he was being
kind enough to allow her to look round. He looked
completely harmless, she thought, and the sun was
shining. He wouldn't do anything to her while the
sun was shining, surely? It was only the shadows in
the street that had put it in her mind to be cautious
in the first place.

To her surprise there was a door in the wall and he
led the way inside, saying proudly that these were the
Arab baths. Megan cast a quick look over the ancient
arches inside and saw that she had indeed come upon
an archaeological site of some kind, a site, moreover,
that was considerably older than even its old surroundings. She remembered that Ibiza, another Balearic
island, had been a colony of the Punic city of Carthage,
and thought that they might well have been in Majorca
too. Then the Moors had owned the island for a long,
long time, just as they had so much of Spain itself.
It wasn't so surprising that they should have left some
of their buildings behind them.

The caretaker began an elaborate pantomime to show how the water had been heated and conducted round the baths. It was, Megan discovered, a typical Arab bath that was worked on the same system as the old Roman baths had been before them and which are now called Turkish baths in the West. The old man dipped up and down, making graphic movements with his hands, and so intent was he on his elaborate explanations that he didn't hear the footsteps approaching, nor did he notice when they were joined by another girl until she spoke to him, a torrent of angry Spanish coming from her brightly lipsticked mouth.

The caretaker stared at her in silence. Megan smiled hopefully at the newcomer and was surprised to find that the girl's interest was in her and not in either the baths or the caretaker.

'I am Inez,' she began in a quaint lisping English that was quite charming. 'Inez de la Navidades. You have heard of me?'

Megan shook her head, silent in the face of such superb confidence.

'But you must have heard of *me*! You are the young English companion of the Señora Vallori, are you not? Then she must have told you all about me. I am the *novia* of Carlos Vallori. How do you say this in English? That we are going steady, no?'

'Are you—are you engaged to Carlos?' Megan asked curiously.

Inez shrugged her shoulders. 'Engaged? Going steady? I am not sure that I understand the difference! These words have a different nuance?'

'Yes,' Megan admitted. 'Yes, they do.'

'Then I must explain it better,' Inez went on. 'I am very close to Carlos. Is that clear enough?'

Megan nodded briefly. She looked curiously at the other girl and thought she was exactly as she would have imagined Carlos' future wife to be. She was beautiful in a flashing, fiery way, with soft, mobile lips that asked to be kissed, and a naturally provocative manner that was charmingly feminine and probably very much admired by the men of her acquaintance.

'How did you know who I am?' Megan asked.

'I saw you walking down here. I could see you were a foreigner and who else would you be? Few tourists come down this way and *they* don't live in the Calle Morey! I saw you coming out of the house. Whatever brought you here, though? Surely you aren't interested in this sort of thing? Anyway, I ran after you to ask you to have tea with me. Will you? It will be nice if we can be friends together as I have no one with whom I can talk about Carlos. You will be my friend, won't you?'

'Of course.'

'Then I shall begin by paying for your ticket here, though I can't think you understood much of what this man had to say about the baths, did you?'

'No,' Megan admitted. 'But he tried to make it interesting. I should like to give him something for himself.'

Inez nodded, frowning. 'If you want to, but he won't expect much—'

'I do want to.'

Megan handed him a coin and was rewarded by a twinkling smile of appreciation. With all the dignity of his race, he picked an orange from one of the trees and handed it to her, murmuring a few words under his breath.

'What does he say?' Megan asked Inez.

The Spanish girl looked amused. 'That you are as beautiful inside as you are on the outside.'

Megan felt herself blushing. 'Oh!' she breathed.

'I think it is probably quite true,' Inez murmured, laughing at Megan's expression. 'Don't you like to receive the compliments?'

'Ye-es,' Megan agreed.

'It is just as Carlos says! You are completely
71

English! How do you enjoy living in the same house as Margot? She is not nearly so English,' Inez added. ' But you have discovered that for yourself?'

' No,' Megan said flatly. ' Of course I haven't been here long, but Señora Vallori isn't an easy person to know.'

' We find her difficult to know, but I thought it might be otherwise with one of her own country-women. She confides in no one, that one!'

' She's very charming, of course,' Megan put in dutifully.

Inez's dark eyes flashed. ' *Very*,' she agreed, trying not to laugh. ' Come, let us go past the Cathedral and have tea together, no? You shall tell me all about yourself and I shall tell you all about Carlos and me!'

Megan had very little choice but to follow the Spanish girl out of the gardens and back into the shadowed street. It was pleasant to have company, though, as they strolled along the cobbled surface, retracing the way that Megan had come from the Calle Morey. Inez knew exactly where to go, finding her way through the narrow maze of streets with the greatest of ease, turning this way and that, past the Bishop's House and the Diocesan Museum, round the magnificent Cathedral itself and past the Almudaina Palace, where General Franco now stays when he comes to the island on state business. Inez pointed out each building with a supreme lack of interest as to what lay inside them.

' I have better things to do,' she said scornfully, ' than to follow the tourists through such places. Carlos is ashamed of my ignorance about our history, but I have no interest in such things. What does it matter what our parents did? I am too busy doing myself.' She turned breathlessly to Megan, her eyes alight with curiosity. ' Where did Carlos meet you? He tells me you know Pilar? Were you staying with her friends in London? Are you a student?'

Megan stopped walking to look in the window of a shop full of wood carvings of Don Quixote and his faithful servant Sancho Panza. They were all hand-made, many of them fashioned to the same pattern, but none the less beautiful for that. Some were made of dark-coloured wood and some in a lighter colour, and their sizes varied from a few inches to several feet high.

'No, I'm not a student. I'm a singer.'

The reaction was everything she could have hoped for. Inez's hands flew up in astonishment, her mouth round with astonishment. 'No? But this is something I have heard nothing about! Tell me all about it immediately. I have never heard anything more interesting!'

Megan gave her a pleased smile, flattered by her exitement. 'I had only just begun *professionally*,' she admitted. 'It's the most marvellous sensation, though! I can't describe how it feels when you stand on a platform and have the whole audience in the hollow of your hand, and you know you can make them feel sad or gay just by the change of timbre in your voice. I've always wanted to be a singer!'

Inez pointed out a café across the road and gave her a little push towards it. 'But in Mallorca there is no difficulty!' she exclaimed. 'It will be easy for you to go on with your career while you are here—'

'No!'

'*Porque no?* There are a hundred night-clubs and places like that where they are always looking for singers! I shall find you a job straight away. My father will help! He owns a great many places of entertainment.'

Megan pushed open the door of the café and sat down at the nearest empty table. She felt suddenly empty of all emotion. It was as though she had been borne along by a balloon that had suddenly been pricked, dropping her with indecent haste back on to

73

the earth. It was only in that moment that she realised the extraordinary thing that had happened to her. She had been happy singing with Tony's band. She had always wanted to sing. And she was going to be perfectly miserable being Señora Vallori's unwelcome companion and having to live in that museum of a house for she didn't know how long!

'I don't know,' she said with difficulty.

'It is clear that this is what you must do!' Inez insisted. 'I shall arrange everything. Leave it all to me!'

'I can't!' Megan burst out. 'I've agreed to be Señora Vallori's companion. She wouldn't like it if I got a job in a night-club! Nor would Carlos!'

'That is a difficulty,' Inez conceded.

Megan summoned up a rather bleak smile. 'C-Carlos doesn't approve of singers.'

Inez screwed up her nose thoughtfully. 'That is true. If it were someone for whom he had no responsibility, he would not mind at all, but in your case he will feel responsible for you—'

'I can look after myself!' Megan snapped.

'But Carlos will not think so,' Inez pointed out reasonably. 'If you are living in his house, he will expect you to be like one of his sisters. He would *never* allow his sisters to sing in public!'

Megan found that she wasn't at all pleased to be classed with Carlos' sisters. It gave her the same uncomfortable feeling that she had when she thought of living in his house as his stepmother's companion. The whole arrangement dismayed her. She didn't want to be anyone's paid companion! She wanted to take to her heels and run as fast as she possibly could, and not just from Señora Vallori and Majorca, but from Carlos too! In fact *especially* from Carlos!

'What am I to do?' she asked, with a helplessness that was unusual in her.

Inez's eyes narrowed. 'You could go back to

England,' she suggested.

Megan shook her head. ' I can't! '

' Because of Carlos?'

The sharpness of the question took Megan unawares. She supposed that it was because of Carlos—in a way. He was relying on her to make his stepmother a little more happy and a little easier to live with, and she wouldn't let him down for anything, which was ridiculous, because Carlos didn't *depend* on anyone, and certainly not on an inexperienced eighteen-year-old like herself.

' And Pilar,' she said, not knowing quite why she did so.

She was rewarded by a wide smile. ' I had forgotten that you know Pilar. It was *she* who persuaded you to look after her mother, no? Ah yes, you are *Pilar's* friend and you can do nothing that would upset her. I understand now why you cannot sing in public while you are here.' With an air of intense satisfaction, Inez turned her head and summoned the young waitress to their table, ordering tea for two and some of the famous Mallorquin puffs, sometimes filled with cream and sometimes not, and dusted with icing sugar. ' But it is a pity, no? I shall tell my father all about you all the same. One never knows what may happen and I should so enjoy knowing a singer! '

Megan opened her mouth to protest that she wasn't any more Pilar's friend than Carlos', but then she thought she was making too much of the whole business and lapsed back into silence.

' So,' Inez's ready tongue broke the silence, ' now I shall tell you about Carlos and me. I have lived in Mallorca all my life. Once I have been to Barcelona, but that is all, and then it was to visit with the Valloris. They have always been so very good to me! Of course when we were children I did not have much to do with Carlos because he is older than the rest of us, but always he was the one I loved the best. Pepe is nice, but he teases all the time and now he is in South America. I think one cannot love anyone who is on the other side of the world? He writes sometimes and tells me I am bad because I don't write back to him!' Inez's eyes flashed with a sudden spurt of temper. 'If he wants to know about me, he can stay here!'

Megan chuckled. 'That's hardly very practical! He has his living to earn!'

Inez shrugged. 'The Valloris don't need any more money. It is only because Carlos insists that he works that Pepe had to go to South America. He could have stayed here and looked after the Vallori almonds, or *something*!' She sounded so passionate on the subject that Megan was amused.

'Doesn't Carlos do that?' she enquired.

'He comes occasionally,' Inez admitted. 'There is a man who looks after the orchards for him. Carlos does nothing himself. *He* doesn't work for his money!'

'But he makes Pepe work?'

'Pepe is the younger son!' Inez said meaningly.

Megan refrained from saying that she had thought she was going to hear about Carlos. She eyed Inez thoughtfully, noting the faintly sulky look that came and went round the full, kissable mouth. The thought occurred to her that the Spanish girl was rather spoilt, and she was amused by the thought. Hadn't that been exactly what people had always said about *her*?

'Do you like Pepe better than Carlos?' she asked aloud, languidly, as though it were of no real interest to her.

Inez flushed. 'Of course not! Pepe is only a boy. Carlos is a man!'

Megan nearly laughed at the Spanish girl's tone of voice, but something prevented her. 'When Pepe comes home he will be a man,' she pointed out.

'But not like Carlos!' Inez denied. 'That was what I was going to tell you about. When Pepe had gone it was so dull here. You have no idea what it was like!

There were a few parties, but nothing that I could interest myself in. Almost everything here is for the tourists—my father works for the tourist industry—and there is hardly anything for people of good family on the island.' She sighed. 'That was when I really got to know Carlos! You have no idea how kind he can be! He was staying at the farm for a few days and I told him that he had managed to ruin my whole life by sending Pepe away *and* taking Pilar and Isabel to Barcelona to live!' She frowned, remembering her former misery. 'He said that it would never do for me to be unhappy and he put on a party especially for me, and called *often* at my parents' house just to see me. It was natural that I should fall in love with him, don't you think? Well, I did! And I think he meant me to because my family is quite as good as his, and he has to marry sooner or later, doesn't he?'

Megan chewed her lower lip thoughtfully. 'I—I suppose so.'

'*Suppose?*' Inez sounded annoyed. 'Carlos understands his responsibilities very well. It is necessary that he should marry and have a son to carry on the family name—'

'Pepe could do that,' Megan objected.

'*Pepe!* That wouldn't be at all the same!' Inez's dark eyes held a tragic look that looked as if it might well brim over into tears. 'Pepe has no money of his own. All the Vallori estates and businesses were inherited by Carlos. Some of them belonged to *his* mother, you understand. Anyway, although his father loved his English wife, Pepe didn't stand a chance when it came to the inheritance.'

'And what about Carlos' stepmother?' Megan knew that she shouldn't enquire into a matter which was absolutely no business of hers, but she was intrigued to know the exact situation between the Señora and her stepson and whether she was still as jealous of him as she had been when he had been a small boy.

Inez raised her eyebrows. 'Carlos takes care of her.'

'Didn't her husband leave her *anything*?' Megan asked in astonishment.

'But of course not!' Inez sounded startled and patronising, both at the same moment. 'Margot has everything she needs. If he had left her any part of the Vallori estate she would have given it to Pepe and that would have been the beginning of the break-up of the Vallori empire. He would have hated that, and so would Carlos!'

Megan swallowed. 'Do they own much property?' She hesitated, catching herself up as she thought about the impropriety of her questioning Inez like this. 'I mean, surely there must be more than enough for them all?'

'Carlos is one of the richest men in Spain,' Inez said judiciously. 'You see what a good thing it would be for me to marry him?'

'I suppose so,' Megan agreed.

'But, Megan, if I married him I should be rich too!'

'There's more to marriage than that,' Megan said. She was beginning to think that her role as Inez's confidante and friend was going to be a rather trying one. 'Won't Carlos expect you to be in love with him?'

Inez wrinkled up her nose, looking highly put out. 'But I told you! I am in love with Carlos! I want to marry him very much and he wants to marry me. If—If he has other friends, that is no concern of mine!'

Megan gave her an anxious look. 'Well, if you can look at it that way—' she began. She made a further effort to hide the fact that she found it the most cold-blooded view of marriage that she had heard for a long time, made all the worse in her view because Inez was actually contemplating entering into such a relationship. 'I couldn't stand any husband of mine playing around with anyone else!'

Inez laughed with real amusement. 'But would you know?'

Megan blushed a little. 'I think I would,' she declared. 'In fact I know I should! Not that I should ever marry anyone like Carlos!' she added for good measure.

'No?' Inez still looked amused. 'Perhaps not,' she agreed. 'You are too prim and too English for a *juerguista* like Carlos. I think you would be frightened if he paid court to you! You would not like it that he takes what he wants! It is as well that I am Spanish and understand these things!' She consciously preened herself, smiling maliciously at Megan. 'Am I not right?'

Megan's eyes filled with tears. She made a play of drinking the last of the tea, remembering that Carlos had kissed her and that he had said that he hadn't disliked it, but what had her reactions been? Not the first, brief thrill of being close to him, but afterwards, when she had finally been allowed to go to her room and climb into the bed that had been Carlos' when he was a boy? She had thought about it from every possible angle, or so she had thought. Now she was not so sure. She had thought all the time as though she were the only woman in the world and, of course, she was not. Even Inez admitted that Carlos had other female friends, and she was hoping to marry him! But, for that short moment, Carlos had been the only man in the world for her. No one else had ever aroused that feeling of wonder and exultancy within her before. Perhaps no one ever would again!

'Probably,' she said at last. 'Even when I marry I want to keep my independence—'

'*Claro!*' Inez nodded vigorously. 'That is very English! In Spain we want to be looked after by our men.' She giggled. 'It is so much more comfortable!' she added languidly. 'If you don't believe me, ask Margot! She is more Spanish in that way than we are!'

Megan couldn't imagine herself doing anything of the sort. She didn't know why, but the thought of Carlos marrying Inez depressed her. She thought the Spanish girl was too light a character to find happiness with Carlos, but then she knew very little of Spanish ways. Probably Inez would be content enough, but Carlos—? What happiness would he have? *It was none of her business*, she reminded herself. Carlos was well able to look after his own interests. Only, somehow, the nagging ache of worry about him wouldn't go away.

Inez walked home with her so that she wouldn't get lost. 'I want to come anyway,' the Spanish girl confided, ' because my parents are coming to dinner with Margot tonight and I want to explain to her why I won't be there. I am promised to another party,' she added by way of explanation, ' and Carlos won't hear of my breaking a previous engagement—even for him!'

She rushed up the stairs ahead of Megan, pushing her way into the gallery, her high heels tapping importantly on the marble floor.

' Tia Margot?'

A sleepy voice answered her from within and Inez hurried into the small sitting room, a flood of Spanish falling from her lips. Megan followed more slowly, giving her eyes time to grow accustomed to the comparative darkness of the interior by pausing and looking at the stiff paintings of Carlos' ancestors. She paused in front of one of a woman that was plainly more modern than all the rest.

' That is my mother,' Carlos' voice said behind her shoulder.

' I thought it must be,' she managed, a little embarrassed to be caught looking at the portrait. She turned back, studying the representation before her with greater care. The first Señora Vallori had been a striking-looking woman. She had the same leaf-green eyes as Carlos and a slightly cynical expression that caught at Megan's ready sympathy. It was sad that she had been parted from her son before she had been able to see him grow to manhood.

'I am said to favour her in my looks,' Carlos drawled slowly. 'Perhaps you don't agree?'

Megan stared up into the painted eyes. 'Why isn't your stepmother's painting here too?' she asked.

'My father preferred to have it in the Barcelona house,' he answered indifferently. 'Do you think I ought to have it brought back here?'

Megan shook her head. 'This is your mother's house,' she said.

He looked at her with renewed interest. 'That is how I feel,' he said. 'But Margot is probably right, I am too inclined to make the house a memorial to a woman I never knew—'

'But you did know her!'

'Not I, the boy who knew her is as dead as she is, and a good thing too! Now that Margot has decided to live here, the house will once again be used by the living, as it ought to be.' His lips twisted into a cynical expression that was the image of his mother's. 'It is time the Valloris laid their ghosts, or not even the intrepid English will come and visit us here!' His laughter mocked her as much as himself. 'May she rest in peace!'

CHAPTER VI

Megan settled into the ways of the Vallori household more speedily than she had thought possible during those long first days when everything had seemed strange to her. She still thought of that first dinner party with something like a shudder, when Inez's parents had come to dinner and had showed their disapproval for herself so plainly. She had thought at first that it had been because she was English and, because she spoke no Spanish and they very little English, they had done no more than smile at one another which had inevitably led to a certain stiffness. Then she had become conscious that they disapproved of her clothes and were discussing her freely amongst themselves. She was wearing an evening trouser suit that flashed in the light and which suited her. Her first reaction had been one of hurt and then she had been angry.

Señora Vallori had smiled at her across the table. 'You should hide your feelings better,' she had said in an aside. 'We don't want our friends to think of you as just another English tourist, do we? *They* are apt to wear trousers too.'

'I thought everyone did nowadays,' Megan had replied evenly.

'Not in Spain!' her hostess had said comprehensively.

'I have seen young girls wearing them in Barcelona,' Carlos had put in.

'*Spanish* girls?' the entire family had demanded, horrified.

'Spanish girls,' he had insisted, 'and not all of them looked as well as Megan does in them. Too much bottom and too little leg!' He had watched the colour mount into Megan's cheeks and had laughed unkindly.

' Isn't there an expression in England about whether it is men or women who wear the trousers?'

Megan had not worn trousers again, either in the house or out of it. On the other hand, she had learned not to mind Señora Vallori's pinpricks and resigned herself to the fact that whatever she did was not destined to find much favour in that quarter.

She set about refurnishing the small sitting-room, enlisting the help of Inez to translate for her in the shops. She enjoyed choosing some English type chairs in which even Carlos could lounge in comfort, some brightly coloured rugs that helped with the winter draughts, and a modern gas heater in front of which they could all toast themselves without being asphyxiated by charcoal fumes. When she had finished, she felt that there was still something lacking, but Señora Vallori was quite content with her efforts, so she kept her doubts to herself.

She was standing in the middle of the room eyeing the bare rooms with some dissatisfaction, when Carlos found her. He stood in the doorway, watching her for a long moment.

' Well,' he drawled, ' haven't you spent enough money on the room yet?'

Megan lifted her head indignantly. ' It didn't cost very much,' she protested.

' I have just been paying the bills,' he told her. ' Like all women, you obviously have no idea of how much money you can get through in a short time! However, my stepmother is pleased with the results, and I suppose that is all that matters!'

Megan's eyes widened. ' But truly, I know the chairs were costly, but the rugs were extraordinarily cheap—or at least, I thought so! I don't believe you could have done much better!' she ended defiantly.

His dark green eyes watched her closely, but not, she thought, with any pleasure. ' I don't like changes,' he said.

Her mouth twitched with amusement. 'It was you who said the Vallori ghosts should be laid to rest,' she reminded him.

'So I did. Well, Miss Impertinence, how much more money do you need to finish off this room?'

Megan shook her head slowly. 'No money. I was just thinking that the walls look bare. May I—may I look round the other rooms and hang some of the pictures in here?'

'Which pictures?' he demanded.

Megan hesitated. She would have liked to have hung his mother's portrait over the fireplace in the place of honour, but she knew that he would never allow her to move it from the gallery. There were other pictures in the house though that she liked: modern, colourful paintings that appealed to her imagination even while she knew very little about them.

'There's one in the dining-room—' she began.

He laughed sardonically. 'Move it if you like,' he said.

'May I really?' She was inordinately pleased. 'Can we move it now and see what it looks like? I love the colours in it! The rugs will pick up some of them too as they have the same red in them.' She grinned at him, delighted. 'It's just the touch I needed!'

'Indeed?' he said dryly.

She looked at him uncertainly. 'You don't mind, do you?' she pleaded.

'No, I don't mind.' He gave her an amused glance. 'I think your taste impeccable, *pequeña*, but I don't want you to be disappointed when my stepmother wishes to banish the picture back to the dining-room again.'

'Oh!' Megan exclaimed. 'Perhaps she won't notice?' she suggested.

'Original paintings by Paul Klee are usually noticed!'

'Oh,' she said again. 'I didn't know it was valuable!'

He smiled. 'Does it make you love it any more?'

She shook her head. 'I don't know much about art,' she admitted. 'But if I did, I hope I shouldn't be mercenary about it!'

He laughed out loud. 'You know what you like!' he accused her.

'I suppose so,' she murmured. 'But I may still move it, mayn't I?'

'If you like,' he said indifferently. 'If Margot doesn't object.'

His stepmother made no comment at all about the picture when Megan called her to have a look at the finished room. She sat in one of the chairs and approved the warmth from the new fire.

'I think it is more comfortable,' she said in her cool voice. 'It will take some getting used to, of course —this house has always been so unwelcoming and cold somehow. I don't like red myself, but I suppose I shall have to put up with it.'

Carlos straightened the picture over the fireplace with a careless finger. 'As there is only a touch of red in the carpets, I take it you like the whole effect?' he pressed her.

Señora Vallori shrugged. 'I'm not particularly interested. You know I'm only living here because you say I must! It doesn't matter to me what you do to the house!'

'Not even if we have the new bathroom installed?' he asked in frighteningly polite tones.

'I prefer to be reasonably civilised,' Margot answered him. 'Your father liked me to be comfortable.'

Carlos' eyes met hers in a long, level look. 'I'm not prepared to discuss your living in England again,' he said abruptly. 'If you don't like it here, Margot, you can live in any one of my other houses, but *not* in England.'

Señora Vallori got to her feet in a single sinuous movement. 'You always were a selfish person,' she said smoothly. 'I don't think you've ever considered anyone but yourself in your whole life!'

Carlos shrugged easily. 'Probably not,' he said.

Megan stood very still, hoping not to call attention to herself, for she couldn't help but be embarrassed by this exchange between the two Valloris. But her very silence made Margot angrier than ever.

'As for you,' she turned on Megan, 'you needn't think that I agreed to having you here. What did Carlos offer you in return for spying on me?'

'N-nothing,' Megan stammered.

'That is enough!' Carlos said sharply. 'Whatever you may think, Margot, I will not have you insulting a guest under my roof.'

'*Your* roof? Can't you think of anything else?'

Carlos put a gentle hand on her shoulder. 'Cheer up, darling,' he said lightly. 'You'll have to get used to it in the end.'

'Never! It's so unfair!'

Carlos' mouth twisted into a wry smile. 'Life is unfair, my dear, but don't take it out on Megan. Our quarrels are nothing to do with her!'

Margot hid her face in her stepson's broad shoulder. 'I miss him so much!' she whispered.

'We all do,' Carlos soothed her.

Megan would have slipped out of the room, but when she went towards the door, Carlos shook his head at her. 'Don't go, Megan. I wish to speak to you.'

Señora Vallori pushed herself away from Carlos. There was a glint of tears in her eyes, but she was also smiling. 'I don't suppose you will need me,' she said with all her usual calm. 'I think I'll go to my room for a while.'

She hurried out of the room, slamming the door shut after her. Megan jumped at the sound, wondering at her own nervousness. She threaded her fingers together, not looking at Carlos at all. It had not been her fault that Señora Vallori had broken down in her presence, but she wished that she hadn't because she was still a stranger to the whole family.

'Why don't you let her go to England and see what it's like for herself?' she asked when she could stand the silence no longer.

'That is hardly your business.'

She peeped at him through her eyelashes. 'I don't like being called your spy,' she said.

'Why not? You know it isn't true.'

Megan wiped her hands on the sides of her skirt, looking very young and vulnerable. 'Why did you bring me here?' she asked abruptly.

He smiled. 'Do I have to have an ulterior reason?'

'No, but your stepmother doesn't want me here. She doesn't need a companion, whatever you and Pilar say. I don't think she particularly likes me, or—or anyone young.'

'And you are very young?'

She thought he was teasing her. 'Not *very* young,' she denied with dignity, 'but too young for your stepmother to confide in.'

Carlos looked amused. 'I don't suppose Margot has ever confided in anyone of her own sex,' he commented. 'Do you want to go back to England and the perils of your life in London? Is that it, *amada*?'

Megan licked her lips. She was shocked to discover that it was the last thing she wanted. On the contrary, the idea of going away and never seeing Carlos again gave her a sinking feeling that alarmed her. *Carlos!* Carlos, who regarded her as a child to be protected from herself and the seamier side of life for no other reason than that she was about the same age as his half-sisters and had appealed to his sense of responsibility.

'I—I don't want to go away.'

He raised an eyebrow, considering this confession. 'Good,' he said. 'It would be a mistake to let Margot frighten you away.' He put a finger under her chin and lifted her head to see her face the better. 'Don't worry if you don't immediately please my stepmother. It isn't she who is employing you.'

'No,' Megan agreed, sighing. 'But I don't seem to have any real job here. I—I must have something to do! Carlos, you do see that, don't you?'

His finger moved up her cheek, tracing the line of her jaw. 'Isn't transforming the house enough for you?'

She shook her head, taking the opportunity to back away from him because she liked the touch of his hands against her face too much for her own comfort. 'There isn't anything for me to do, is there?' she said.

'It's an opportunity for you to have the freedom to discover yourself,' he answered. 'Don't you think you might enjoy that?'

'At your expense?' she countered.

His eyes met hers. 'I can afford it.'

'That isn't the point!' she argued.

'Perhaps not,' he admitted. 'It will have to be enough for you, however, that your parents have agreed to your coming and here you will stay until I am ready to let you go home.'

'As your stepmother's companion?' she asked, angry at his light dismissal of any say that she might have in the matter.

'As anything I care to make you!'

Megan gasped and then she laughed. 'You're too arrogant to be true!' she told him. 'What would you do if I decided not to stay?' she added.

'You'll stay!' he told her lightly.

'How do you know?'

He grinned. 'It's a challenge, and I can't see you running away from that!'

Megan could see herself running away only too easily, but she said nothing. 'I must have something to do!' she repeated doggedly.

'All right,' he agreed. 'You can fetch your coat and come with me to the farm. There's always plenty to do over there.'

She eyed him uncertainly, but his attention had already left her. He turned on his heel and walked out of the room, calling over his shoulder: 'Ten minutes! I'll wait for you in the patio.'

She stood there for a long moment, looking after him, and then in a sudden mad rush, she whirled out of the room, up the stairs and into her bedroom to get her coat.

It seemed that Carlos had a car of his own wherever he happened to be. Megan stepped into the comfortable Porsche waiting outside the patio, giving a little wriggle of pleasure as she explored the width of the seat and the ample leg room in front of her. Carlos gave her a sardonic look, but he said nothing, only letting in the clutch, moving the car slowly forward down the narrow street.

He found his way easily on to the ring road that went around the centre of Palma, and they were soon on the main highway going out of the city towards the east.

'Where is your farm?' Megan asked him.

'Between Felanitx and Porto Cristo. We'll turn off this road in a moment and go through Lluchmayor. There's a map in the compartment in front of you, if you want to see for yourself.'

But Megan was content just to be driven through the countryside, enjoying the beauty of her surroundings as they sped along. The windmills stood in clusters over the plain, most of them stationary despite the light wind. Carlos explained that they were really water-wheels, drawing up the water from the depths of the earth to irrigate the numerous farms and small-holdings. 'You'll see them all over the island, but the majority of them are in this area. It looks like an obstacle course for Don Quixote, doesn't it?'

'Perhaps he wasn't the only one to tilt at windmills,' Megan said lazily.

Carlos chuckled. 'Some people do it all their lives,' he agreed.

Megan tilted her head. 'Are you getting at me?' she enquired.

'If the cap fits—!'

'It doesn't. I'm older than you think,' she told him. 'Sometimes it doesn't do to rate everybody's age by the number of years they have lived. Experience comes into it too. I haven't lived the protected existence of a Spanish girl. I'm older than Inez, for example.'

A smile played on his lips. 'I wonder,' he said.

'In what way is she more experienced than me?' she demanded.

'In the ways of pleasing a man,' he suggested.

Megan was silent. She had a vivid mental picture of Inez flirting with Carlos, in his arms and being kissed by him. It was hard to believe, she granted him, that Inez, with that eminently kissable mouth, had never been kissed. And whom else would she kiss, if not Carlos whom she was destined to marry? Even her parents would not object to that.

'There are *other* things!' Megan said at last.

'Not for the average Spanish girl,' he observed dryly.

Megan took a deep breath. 'I'm glad that I have other things on my mind!' she claimed fervently.

Carlos laughed. 'But then you are very young!' he teased her.

It was the kind of circular argument that she hated, but anything was better than dwelling on the picture of Carlos and Inez together. Megan drew herself up coquettishly.

'That's all you know!' she said.

' I do know ! ' he drawled.

Megan blushed. ' But that wasn't you I kissed !
That was the boy you said was dead and gone ! ' she
protested.

The sound of his laughter roared round her. ' Oh,
Megan ! ' he exclaimed.

' But it's true ! '

' Then heaven help you when you get around to
kissing a man in earnest ! ' he shot at her.

' Perhaps I never will,' she said uncomfortably.

He put a hand over hers, squeezing her fingers in
his. ' Grow up quickly, *niña*.'

She sighed. ' I have grown up, only you won't see it.
I'm older now than Inez will ever be ! Only Spanish
women are more *obvious*—'

' *De Veras?* If you talked like this to that Tony of
yours I am not surprised he thought you were willing
to experiment a little ! '

' He didn't think me a child ! ' Megan defended
herself.

' But he managed to frighten you all the same,'
Carlos reminded her. ' Why be in such a hurry?'

Megan would have liked to have denied that she
was, but she lacked the courage to say anything more.
Inez was the girl he wanted for his wife. She would
do well to remember that ! She could worry all she
liked because she knew that Inez was too shallow and
circumscribed to hold his interest for long, but *it
wasn't any of her business* ! Inez was the one who was
going to be loved and cherished because she would be
the mother of his children and would bear the proud
name of Vallori. Megan took a deep, strangled breath,
for in that moment she knew that she *hated* Inez !
Her mouth went dry at the thought. Inez had everything she wanted for herself, and she simply wasn't
goon enough for Carlos. Megan clenched her fists and
then made herself relax. She was in love with Carlos
—not Carlos, the lost and lonely boy, but Carlos the

man who saw her only as a pleasant child who would one day grow up and go back to England, out of his life for ever.

'I didn't mean to say anything disparaging about Inez, or—or Spanish women,' she said finally.

His dark green eyes flicked over her. 'You could learn a lot from the gentle ways of someone like Inez. A man likes to relax in the company of women, not continually raking over the coals over which one of them is master.'

She turned her face away so that he wouldn't see how badly he had hurt her. 'I try to conform,' she said wearily. 'Only I don't know what's expected of me.'

'Nobody expects anything except that you should enjoy yourself. Margot tells me you have a driving licence. You can borrow one of the cars and get out and about whenever you want to. The only stipulation I make is that you tell either Margot or myself which direction you are going in. Some of the roads over the mountains are steep and dangerous and if you get stuck, I want to know where to find you.'

'I've never driven on the right,' she said.

'I'll give you a try out before I allow you to go out by yourself,' he promised her. 'I want to see for myself if you really can drive.'

She smiled cheekily across at him. 'I can drive,' she said.

'Then you've nothing to worry about,' he answered.

When they left the main road they came immediately into the agricultural area of the island. The narrow road rambled through the almond orchards, looking exceptionally pretty in the sunshine. The delicate shaded blossom covered the trees, drifts of pale pink and white, wherever one looked. Lit up by sunlight, it danced in frothy perfection in the light breeze, more fragile than any other blossom Megan had ever seen, she thought it more beautiful even than the apple and cherry blossom she was accustomed to.

'Before summer holidays became the usual thing,' Carlos told her, 'most visitors used to come to Mallorca in February to see the almond blossom. The island is at its prettiest at this time of year.'

'Like George Sand and Chopin?'

Carlos smiled wryly. 'Not exactly. I don't think they were in the usual run of tourists, even in those days.'

'Perhaps not,' Megan agreed. 'But I should like to see where Chopin actually stayed and composed some of his music. I think I'll go to Valldemosa first of all!'

'You'd better take Inez with you,' Carlos said lazily. 'You can explain to her on the way who Chopin was.'

Megan felt affronted on the Spanish girl's behalf. 'I expect she already knows,' she said mildly.

But Carlos only grinned. It was odd, Megan thought, that he should be so certain that Inez wouldn't know such a thing, and yet he didn't mind a bit. Couldn't he see that his wife and he would have few interests in common? She could only think that he didn't intend to talk much with his wife at all. Probably he would only expect her to look beautiful and to be the mother of his children. When he wanted conversation he would go elsewhere, to the men of his acquaintance and to other women. It was odd to think that he would be satisfied with so little.

Felanitx was practically deserted. The long, shuttered, winding streets were empty except for the occasional horse-drawn cart, or housewife, well wrapped in shawls, doing her shopping. A few old men sat in the sun in the central square, watching a group of children as they played in the entrance to the church, rolling up and down the imposing steps that led up to the door, laughing and joking with the priests as they went in and out, busy about their pastoral duties. There was no immediate sign that this was an important agricultural town, the centre of the wine-growing district, and with an important factory where they made pork preserves. It looked like a town that had been passed by in modern times, a place that had nothing better to do but sleep in the early spring sunshine.

Carlos waited impatiently while a farm-cart clattered down the empty street towards him. The driver raised his cap high above his head as he passed, the shod hooves of the horse slipping on the rough cobbles. Carlos acknowledged the salute with a brief nod, and the car shot forward, past the long line of closely shuttered windows and firmly closed doors.

The farm was not far from Felanitx. The entrance led straight off the road, little more than a cart-track between the blossom-laden almond trees and the neat stone walls that marked out one orchard from another. The house was large and old. The ancient pantiles were badly in need of repair and someone had patched them with large, heavy stones that were also supposed to protect the roof from the wind. A few hens scratched a living in the yard in front of the house. At night, they shared the sheds that took up the whole of the ground floor of the house with the horse, a couple of cows, a few donkeys, and the farm-carts. The living quarters were reached up by a single flight of marble steps that rose majestically to the first floor.

A young girl came running out of the house, a broad smile on her face. With a naturalness that Megan could only envy, she kissed Carlos lightly on the cheek, laughing at his greeting. Then, still talking nineteen to the dozen, she came round the car and kissed Megan too, easing her gently out of the car with a smiling concern for her comfort.

'This is Rosita, the daughter of my farm manager,' Carlos introduced the girl.

'*Buenas dias*,' the girl said shyly. She stood with her back to the car, her arms akimbo, surveying Megan with an unconcealed interest. Occasionally, she threw

94

a question to Carlos, laughing at his answers.

'She wants to know if you would like some tea—among other things?' Carlos translated.

Megan smiled. 'What other things?' she demanded.

His dark green eyes mocked her. 'That would be telling,' he teased her. 'Do you want some tea?'

She nodded eagerly. 'I'd love some.'

They mounted the marble steps to the darkened room above. Rosita made a great clattering noise as she opened the shutters, allowing a faint ray of sunshine to intrude into the gloomy atmosphere.

'*Siéntese por favor,*' she smiled at Megan, pointing out a tattered red velvet chair that stood in lonely state in front of the fireplace.

Megan sat down quickly, mildly relieved when Carlos drew up another chair, sitting down beside her. Rosita stood casually beside him, making sure that he was comfortable and throwing out little titbits of local gossip for his amusement. When she finally went away to make the tea, Carlos lit himself a cigarette and smiled across at Megan.

'I don't think anyone ever comes in here in the normal way,' he said. 'The family are very hard-working and have little time for sitting. It's in your honour that we've been put in here.'

'Did you tell her that I'm only your stepmother's companion?' Megan asked him.

'No,' he said abruptly.

The tea was tasteless and almost cold. Rosita prodded a single tea-bag in an enormous and very pretty teapot with a teaspoon as though she hoped this would somehow make it stronger. The little honey cakes that she said her mother had made that morning were delicious and Rosita was plainly delighted when Carlos helped himself to a second one, hopefully pushing the plate closer to Megan.

As soon as he had finished, Carlos rose to his feet, saying something in Spanish to Rosita.

' I must go and have a word with Rosita's father,' he added to Megan. ' Can you amuse yourself for a few moments?'

' Of course,' Megan said.

She went with him down the stairs and out into the yard. Carlos strode off down one of the rutted pathways, leaving her to her own devices. It was hard to know what to do, for she had no idea how long he would be, but the sight of the pink and white trees in the orchards tempted her to take a closer look at them. She walked a short way along the cart-track down which they had come from the road, pausing every now and then to look at the wild flowers and the prickly pear, with its curious scarlet fruits hanging on to the spiked, fleshy leaves.

She came to the road sooner than she had expected and sat on one of the stone walls, swinging her legs in front of her. The electricity wires passed over her head, humming faintly in the light breeze. There wasn't a single car in sight, although she judged that she could see several miles along the road in either direction. But, after a few moments, the stones began to stick into her and she jumped off the wall, leaning instead against one of the posts that held up the wires.

The silence was broken by a group of young people coming home from market, their chatter filling the still air. Megan took a step forward as their horse plodded past her, wanting to see what they had bought, but the cart was empty except for the family of children.

As they passed, one of them pointed to the post she had been leaning against and shouted to the others. There was a chorus of appreciation from inside the cart, as it turned off the road again, disappearing down another of the tracks that led off the road. Megan turned to see what they had been looking at and saw a red and yellow bill stuck to the post. But it was not this that surprised her. It was what the bill advertised, for there, written in both Spanish and English, were the words:

TONY STARLIGHT—IN MAJORCA FOR A SEASON OF SONG—COME AND LISTEN TO THE BAND!

It was impossible to believe! Tony, *her* Tony, was here in Majorca!

CHAPTER VII

Megan's heart thumped within her. She had always thought Starlight to be a ridiculous name for a man like Tony to have assumed, but he had insisted that with a commonplace first name like Tony his last name had to be something memorable and romantic, something that would appeal to the young girls as he imagined the highwaymen had in the days when the gentlemen of the road had been well known the length and breadth of England.

Tony Starlight! It was a chance, a second chance, she had never expected to have. It had all seemed so simple to give up her singing and to come to Majorca, but now she knew she couldn't stay with the Valloris for ever, and what was she going to do then? Somehow, she thought, she would find a way to see Tony again and ask his advice. True, he wouldn't be particularly pleased to see her after their last meeting, but he was a professional before he was anything else and she thought he would be glad to employ her again on purely professional terms.

So intent was she on her thoughts that she failed to notice that Carlos had finished talking with his manager and had come back to the car. He was almost on top of her before she realised that he had come to fetch her, and she was so nervous that he might see the advertisement for Tony's band that she jumped and almost ran down the cart-track towards him.

'Well, well, *hija*, have you missed me so much?'

She came to a stumbling stop, blushing. 'Don't be silly!' she said sharply. 'It's only been a few minutes!'

He looked at her curiously. 'What are you trying to hide?' he demanded.

'I?' She was the picture of innocence. 'N-nothing!'

'I am disappointed!'

Megan could feel herself blushing again and she hurried into the car before he noticed that he had embarrassed her and would wonder why. She was very conscious of him though as he got in beside her. His gaze swept over her, his eyes amused and mocking.

'Have you decided you are too young for the arts of dalliance?'

The blush burned in her cheeks. 'No,' she breathed.

'Something is the matter,' he went on. 'You're like a cat on hot bricks!'

She twisted her fingers together. 'You should have brought Inez with you,' she said.

His amusement grew visibly. 'What makes you say that?'

'*She* isn't too young for you!'

'And you are? Is that what you are trying to say?'

She shook her head, wishing she had kept a still tongue in her head. 'It isn't important,' she said. 'I only meant that Inez would have expected you to take her. You shouldn't hurt people out of carelessness.'

His green eyes grew darker. 'What makes you think Inez is hurt?'

'I don't know,' she admitted. 'But Inez l-likes you, and she's everything you want in a woman—'

'Indeed?' he said coldly.

Megan bit her lip. 'You said yourself that she knows how to please a man,' she muttered defensively.

'Perhaps you've never tried,' he taunted her.

'I've never wanted to!'

He put out a hand and touched her hair. 'Not even with that Tony of yours?'

She started guiltily. 'T-Tony was my employer,' she said with dignity.

'That didn't stop him kissing you, I seem to remember,' he reminded her. She wished that he wouldn't touch her and retreated as far away from him as she could, terrified that he would guess that Tony was in

Majorca and, even worse, that he would know that she had fallen in love with him, unasked and without any reason. If he knew how much she wanted to fling herself into his arms, what would he think of her then?

'Tony was angry,' she said helplessly. The pressure in the back of her throat told her that she was near to tears. 'He never tried to kiss me before.'

His fingers touched her neck and the line of her jaw. 'Do you miss him?' he asked very gently.

She shook her head. Unbidden tears filled her eyes and she blinked them back quickly. 'I don't know,' she said. 'I have to do *something*. I'll always have to earn my own living, and I sing better than I do anything else.'

'You'll marry and then it will be your husband's privilege to look after you—'

'He may not have any money!' Megan protested. 'I—I might prefer to support myself!'

'Then you had better not marry a Spaniard!' he smiled at her.

'I don't intend to!' she retorted promptly.

His green eyes lit up dangerously. 'I shouldn't be too sure of that,' he warned her. His fingers moved down the line of her jaw and traced the shape of her lips. 'I don't think the cold Englishman one hears so much about would be any match for you. He wouldn't kiss you like this—and like this!'

His lips touched her face briefly and then clung to her lips. The tears welled up in her eyes and brimmed over, adding a salty flavour to the kiss. Megan gasped and struggled urgently against him, but his arms only held her the tighter until she could scarcely breathe. With a murmur of surrender, she came closer to him, aware only of the burning excitement within her.

'*Alma mia!*' he whispered.

Megan wrenched herself away from him, smiling tremulously as she did so. 'I think I am too young after all,' she said. 'I was right, you should have brought Inez with you.'

Carlos put his hands on her shoulders and gave her a little shake. 'Have it your way, *hija—for now*. You can't play around with the fire of the dragon's breath, though, and not expect to be changed. But I can wait. I can wait a long, long time, *queridissima!*'

'It was the dragon's breath, wasn't it?' she almost pleaded with him. 'It—it was only *flirting!* I don't think you ought to kiss me any more,' she added quaintly. 'I didn't like it.'

'Oh, Megan! Little liar! I have only to whisper *enamorada, amanta—*'

The colour rushed into her cheeks. 'But it doesn't mean anything!' she said in a suffocated whisper.

He sighed. 'Perhaps you are too young after all,' he agreed stiffly. 'I'm sorry if I frightened you.'

Megan winced just as if he had hit her. 'Please take me home!' she burst out

He put a hand under her chin, forcing her to look at him. 'What do you want, Megan? Someone like your Tony who will never stand on his own feet as long as he lives? Even he frightened you, if you remember!'

'I told you, he was angry. He wouldn't kiss me against my will just for the fun of it!'

'No?' he asked sardonically.

'No.' She swallowed. 'He'd *ask—*'

He shrugged his shoulders, losing all patience with her. 'If you want to be asked, my dear, you are younger than I thought! If I want your kisses, I'll take them, with or without your consent. Between a man and a woman, any man worth his salt is the master! You'd do well to remember that!'

'But it isn't between a man and a woman!' The tears were coming fast and furiously now. Megan sniffed desperately, but nothing seemed to make her feel any better. 'It isn't like that with us!'

His expression was hard and unyielding. She peeped at him through her tears and then wished that she hadn't. He was as hard as granite and he had only to touch her and she would be lost for ever. Silently, he handed her a handkerchief and watched her as she made a pathetic attempt to blow her nose and halt the humiliating tears that streamed down her face.

'I'm sorry!' she said.

He smiled. 'If you cry any harder you'll put the dragon's fire out once and for all!'

Megan felt completely wretched. 'I might have known you'd say something *horrid!*'

'Wasn't that the idea?'

She sniffed. 'What was the idea?'

'To damp down the fire,' he drawled.

'Oh, *I hate you!*'

'Wasn't it the idea?'

'No! I *don't know!* No, of course it wasn't! I never cry! Only, when I do, I can't stop! It's got nothing to do with you anyway!'

She saw that he was laughing at her and she became crosser than ever, shredding his handkerchief between angry fingers. He took it from her, putting it back into his pocket.

'Besides,' Megan went on, feeling suddenly better, 'I don't believe in dragons.'

Carlos grinned. 'You can see the skin of ours, any time you want to, in the museum,' he told her.

'But not running around free!'

'Didn't you feel his breath against your cheek?' he asked her.

She thought of denying that she had felt anything at all. He *couldn't* know how she had felt, or about the burning excitement that his touch aroused inside her!

'Lots of people kiss and forget,' she said.

His eyes held hers for a long moment. 'Will you forget?'

Megan refused to answer. Then she said, 'I don't think talking about dragons is much excuse for—for *kissing on the side*!'

His laughter was very disturbing. 'Are you saying that you enjoyed it after all?' he demanded.

She held her head high, refusing to meet his dark, leaf-green eyes. 'I don't think it's at all gallant of you to ask,' she reproved him. 'Not that I expect you to be gallant!' she added darkly. 'And I wish you wouldn't look at me like that!'

A smile played round his lips. 'I'll look at you in any way I like,' he drawled.

The sun was in their eyes as they drove back to Palma. The glaring light hit the windscreen, almost blinding them. It was particularly difficult to see the home-going carts as they drove slowly along the main road, clip-clopping their way down the middle of the road. Carlos drove in silence, concentrating all his attention on the road ahead of him. Megan tried to do the same, but her thoughts refused to follow the line she was pushing them along, coming back again and again to the moment when Carlos had kissed her.

'Inez says there is a fan museum near here,' she said aloud.

'A very fine one,' Carlos agreed. 'Do you want to see it?'

She shook her head. 'I'll come with Inez. She has a collection of them herself which she has promised to show me some time.'

'Then she must certainly show you the fan museum,' he said dryly.

She cast a swift look beneath her eyelashes. 'I can imagine Inez using a fan, can't you? She has such pretty movements.' She sighed. 'I wouldn't know what to do with it!'

'You must get Margot to teach you!'

'Does she use a fan?' Megan couldn't have said why

103

she was so surprised, but she had never thought of anyone but a Spanish-born lady mastering the intricate art of opening and shutting a fan in a single satisfying, rustling movement. ' I've never seen her with one.'

' It's the winter now,' he said. ' In the summer it's a different story when everyone is trying to keep cool. All the young men will vie with each other to present you with a fan of your own then.'

She refrained from pointing out that she didn't know any young men in Majorca, let alone any who would want to give her anything.

' I think I'll ask Inez for one of hers,' she said.

He shrugged. ' Just as you like.'

Only it wasn't as she liked! If she had what she liked, she knew exactly how it would be. Carlos *himself* would give her a fan, the most beautiful fan in the whole of Spain! And she would know from instinct how to use it, to flatter him with it, and flirt with him a little, and make him aware of herself as a mature, fully grown up woman who would know just as well as Inez how to please him!

She gave herself a little shake, dismissing the dream. A strong dose of hard reality was what she needed, she thought, and that brought her back to Inez.

' Have you kissed her often?' she wanted to know, and was horrified to hear herself asking.

' Kissed whom?' he said. His voice was very withdrawn and she wished more than ever that she hadn't said anything at all.

' I-Inez.'

' There's only one thing that I *never* do,' he began, his voice so remote that she thought she would never be warm again.

' What's that?' she asked inevitably. The glare from the sun was hurting her eyes, but in a funny way she was glad of it.

' I never kiss and tell,' he said.

*　　*　　*

Megan didn't see Carlos once in the next three days. It was hard to believe that this was coincidence, seeing that they were both living under the same roof, so she could only think that he was avoiding her. She tried to persuade herself that he wasn't angry with her and that she had behaved better when he had taken her over to the farm than she knew she had. If she had had to be so young and *silly*, she chided herself frequently, why had she had to bring Inez into it? That had been the one unforgivable thing! *That* had been why he had avoided her ever since!

In a half-hearted sort of way, Megan had tried to find out where Tony's band was playing, but there were no notices to be seen in Palma that mentioned his name and she was beginning to think that she had dreamed that he was in Majorca. But then, on the third day, Inez came to call.

' Megan, I have had a brilliant idea!' the Spanish girl squealed excitedly, not even pausing to sit down. ' You know that my father is in the tourist business? I must have told you so! Well, he has a small *hacienda* in the country, on the way to Valldemosa, where he holds barbecues for those who wish to come. It is a very good evening, I can tell you. But, *mire*, there is always a dance that goes on until midnight after the people have eaten. And—' Her voice reached a new peak of excitement—' at the moment, we have an English group making the music!'

Megan's professional interest was aroused. ' Do they have a singer?' she enquired.

Inez shrugged. ' I haven't heard them yet,' she said. ' That is what I was thinking about. We shall go this evening and hear them play and, if everything goes well, *you* can sing with them!'

' Do you think so?' Megan said doubtfully.

' Why not? They are English, I am telling you, so you may already know them?'

Megan swallowed. ' You don't happen to know—?'

'Tony!' Inez produced in triumph. 'That is Antonio, no? Tony Starlight!' She smiled suddenly, her eyes dancing with amusement. 'My father says they are not very good, but he thinks the tourists will like them because they make a great deal of noise!'

Megan sank into the nearest chair, her knees feeling suddenly weak and unable to support her.

'I should have to ask Señora Vallori,' she began, trying to still the flustered excitement that rose within her.

'I will ask her,' Inez decided. 'Tia Margot never refuses me anything!' She threw Megan another, slanting smile. 'I'll tell her not to mention it to Carlos,' she added. 'He doesn't approve of women going to a place of entertainment unescorted and if he came too, he wouldn't allow you to sing!'

'No, he wouldn't,' Megan agreed. The thought of his displeasure made her tremble. 'Though he has no authority over me!'

Inez drew in her breath sharply. 'But you would not defy him, if he was there, would you?' she asked in awe.

'I don't know,' Megan admitted.

'Then you have never seen him angry! *I* would never dare to provoke his anger, not even Tia Margot says anything to him when he is angry. My mother says that once, when Carlos was a boy, he nearly killed Tia Margot in one of his rages. My mother knew his mother and she says Tia Margot should have known better than to disparage her. My mother says that if Tia Margot had gone about it the right way, she could have twisted Carlos around her little finger, but now it is too late. He gives her everything she asks for, of course, but he has never given lovingly to anyone. Perhaps now he never will!'

'When he marries—' Megan began, but Inez stopped her with a look.

'He will be kind to his wife,' the Spanish girl opined

106

realistically. 'She will be a fortunate woman to be married to such a man, but Carlos will never give in to any woman. It is she who will have to give everything to him.'

Megan frowned. It didn't seem to her that Inez would take second place to the man she married She would want to be spoilt and petted, just as she was by her own family.

'I think he'd love her very much,' she said.

Inez laughed and pouted. 'No, no! Carlos will be good to her, but he will never be faithful to any one woman. He will respect her because she will bear his name and his children, but his love is in the tomb with his mother.'

'Inez!'

The Spanish girl laughed, her eyes dancing. 'It is true! But it is not the tragedy you think it to be! Which one of us would refuse to be his wife? *Verdad*, I can hardly wait for him to ask me!'

'I suppose you're in love with him,' Megan said in such flat, dreary tones that she surprised herself.

Inez shrugged. 'A little,' she admitted. 'I am very easily in love! I am both pretty and healthy, so what else should I be?'

Megan could have told her, but she didn't. If she was so much in love with Carlos that it hurt, even to think of him, it didn't mean that every other girl had to feel the same way, not even the girl he was going to marry.

Margot Vallori readily gave her permission for Megan to go to the barbecue with Inez. 'I expect your parents will be there,' she said to Inez, 'and that they will look after you both.'

'Yes, so you mustn't concern yourself about us if we are late home,' Inez told her easily. 'That's why we don't want you to tell Carlos where we are. We don't want him bringing us home before we've begun to enjoy ourselves!'

'I don't think Carlos would want to interfere with your pleasure, Inez,' Margot reproved her.

Inez made a face at her. '*Clara que no!*' she muttered sarcastically. 'You think not, Tia?'

Margot said nothing more on the subject. 'If you want to, you can take my car,' she offered. 'Megan can drive you home, Inez, on the way back here.'

'Carlos wants to see how well I drive before I go out on my own,' Megan reminded her.

'You won't be on your own,' Margot retorted in a voice that brooked no defiance. 'Inez will be with you.'

And so, with Inez in the passenger seat beside her, Megan set out to drive the few miles along the Valldemosa road to the Novidad *hacienda*. Inez, she thought, looked beautiful in a scarlet chiffon dress that billowed about her when she moved. She wished that her own dress had been in the same class, but she had never been able to pay the kind of money that the Spanish girl obviously did. Her own dress was a simple white shift that reached to the floor and which had cost only a few shillings as she had made it herself. Her silver evening sandals were different, however. They had been a present from her parents and she had come to look on them as her good luck charm and had worn them on every occasion she had sung in public since she had had them.

It took all her concentration to drive Margot's tiny Seat through the crowded streets of Palma. The tyres vibrated against the cobbles and the gears were unfamiliar and it seemed very odd to be sitting on the left-hand side of the car. A policeman whistled at her and she realised that she had not noticed him at all, bringing her stream of traffic to a halt, and that scared her. She wished that she had waited for Carlos to take her out a few times before driving alone in this seething maelstrom of traffic.

'You should have turned right there,' Inez said

suddenly.

'But there was no sign to Valldemosa,' Megan protested.

Inez shrugged her shoulders. 'It is quicker, that is all. The sign is on the next road. You can turn there.'

Megan obediently did as she was told, relieved beyond measure to see the traffic thinning out and a clear road ahead of her. In another few minutes they would be out of town and she would have nothing more to worry about until the journey back.

'If Carlos had come with us—' Inez began, and stopped.

'Yes?' Megan prompted her.

'I was only thinking that it will be strange not to have an escort at the dance,' Inez went on sulkily. 'What will I do while you sing?'

Megan felt suddenly cold. 'But surely your family will be there—won't they?' she ended on an uncertain note that dismayed her.

'My *family*?' Inez shuddered at the thought. 'No, no, my family seldom visit the barbecue. The place is very old, you understand. Of course it has all been made quite modern inside, but when there are old walls there is always damp and cold in the winter. In the summer, sometimes we all go and enjoy ourselves, watching the horses race and the flamenco dancers, but in the winter, my family never goes in the winter.'

'Then who organises the barbecue?' Megan asked.

'There is a manager,' Inez explained indifferently. She gave a sudden jump. 'Oh, Megan! I had forgotten all about Señor Valdez! He's bound to tell Papa that I was at the barbecue and what will I do then?'

'Perhaps he won't notice you,' Megan said comfortably.

'Not notice me!' Inez was more put out than Megan had ever seen her. 'You don't know what you are talking about! I never would have come if I had thought of him before! Papa will be very angry with me!'

'But why? It isn't so terrible,' Megan argued. 'It isn't as though you will be completely alone—'

'I don't think you would be acceptable as a chaperone,' Inez interrupted her.

'Why not?'

'We know too little about you. Margot has told my parents a little, you may be sure, but it— Megan, why did you have to behave so *badly* in England?'

The cold feeling tightened its grip around Megan's spine. 'What did Margot say about me?'

'Only what Carlos had told her,' Inez answered. 'She said that you were a singer in a very bad place, and that you only sang there because you knew the man in charge very well and had influence over him. She said that Carlos says you were too young to know what you were getting into, but that you couldn't stay in England any longer because—well, because people were talking about you. We all know that that is why you came to Mallorca! Tia Margot is very concerned about your coming. She says that Carlos will find people talking about him too, when they find that he brought you to his home, and that he thinks his name is too honourable for anyone to think that he would stoop to anything bad, but that he doesn't know human nature!'

Megan's hands shook and she grasped the wheel so tightly that her knuckles showed white in the faint moonlight. She wouldn't have believed that Carlos would have discussed her so freely if Inez's innocent remarks hadn't constituted proof positive. How could he? If he disapproved of her, nobody had asked him to rescue her, or to bring her to Majorca! She could imagine him arrogantly supposing that his name would cover all her misdeeds! Only there hadn't been any misdeeds and she was not in need of his protection!

In fact, if he hadn't *gossiped* about her to his step-mother, nobody in Majorca would have known anything about her!

'I don't think Margot could have understood what Carlos said to her,' she said, astonished that she should sound so calm.

'But she did!' Inez insisted. 'Can you pretend, Megan, that the man who employed you wasn't kissing you when Carlos first saw you? Of course he thought that you had kissed him before!' She paused. 'Had you?' she asked, her curiosity getting the better of her caution.

'No,' Megan said.

'Then why was he kissing you then?'

'I don't know,' Megan sighed. 'The show had gone well and I had gone out into the street because it was stuffy inside. It was snowing and I had forgotten to put my coat on. I was shivering and Tony put his arms round me and kissed me.'

Inez gasped. 'But what a terrible thing to do! No wonder Carlos was shocked!'

'I think it would take more than that to shock Carlos,' Megan said dryly.

'But, Megan, you can't think so! Nobody has ever kissed me! Not even Carlos would do so until after we're officially betrothed—perhaps not until after we are married!'

'I don't want to talk about it,' Megan said abruptly.

'I should think not!' Inez agreed. 'I am glad Carlos would have more respect for me than to—to kiss me *before*—'

'But you know that Carlos kisses other women!' Megan interrupted her, quite suddenly furiously angry.

Inez pouted in silence. 'Has he kissed you?' she asked.

Megan could feel herself blushing. 'Don't you think you ought to concentrate on which way we're going?' she enquired. 'We'll be at Valldemosa in a moment.'

Inez leaned forward, peering out into the darkness. 'You must turn off at the next road,' she directed. 'You can see the gates from here. You see those carved pillars? You go in there.'

Megan turned the little car off the road and parked it neatly between two coaches bearing the names of various travel organisations who had brought their clients from their hotels to the barbecue. A young man, dressed as a cowboy, helped them out of the car and directed them into the courtyard of the old farmhouse. A long fork, with a sausage stuck on the end, was pushed into their hands and they made their way over to the nearest charcoal brazier to heat up their sausages and to receive their glass of *sangria*, a drink made of wine, brandy and lemon juice.

The courtyard was full of excited people, their pale faces made red by the blazing coals around which they huddled eagerly, for the wind was decidedly cold. Megan stood back from the others, sipping her *sangria* and trying to control the cold, clutching sensation that had settled around her stomach. In that moment she decided that she hated Carlos. He had humiliated her in a way she had never known before, not even bothering to tell the truth about her. He must have known that Tony's kiss had meant nothing to her! He must have known that she had been taken by surprise—he *had* known, so why had he lied about it to Margot?

She made a half-hearted gesture of toasting her sausage, giving her full concentration to keeping her place in front of the brazier.

'Hey there! You've been there long enough!' someone said in her ear, and she turned quickly to apologise.

'Tony!' she gulped, not caring that her sausage had fallen off the end of her fork.

'By all that's wonderful!' Tony exclaimed. 'Darling! My lovely Megan Meredith!'

CHAPTER VIII

'Oh, *Tony*!'

His smile was bitter, but at least he was smiling. 'Do I detect a certain change in your feelings for me, Megan my love?'

She took refuge in confusion. 'I don't know what you mean,' she said.

'As feminine as ever!' he accused her.

She sipped nervously at the pretty red liquid in her glass. 'The thing is,' she said with difficulty, 'the Witch's Cauldron wasn't my scene.'

'You're so right, my love! Between you and me, it wasn't mine either. But, as you can see, the boys and I have progressed, even without your help, and here we are, singing nightly and playing for the dance after the barbecue at this respectable dump. Care to join us?'

She took a swift look at him through her eyelashes. 'No funny business?'

'Cross my heart and hope to die!'

'Then I would like to sing with you—just for to-night! I've missed it all so much! You've no idea what it's been like!'

'Well, love, it was your choice. I didn't tell you to go.'

'No, you didn't,' she admitted. 'But you made it inevitable—in a way!'

His smile flashed out. 'Oh, Megan! Are you going to pretend that you didn't want to be kissed?'

'I didn't!' she protested.

He leaned forward, looking at her very closely. 'Funnily enough, I believe you,' he pronounced. 'What's it all about, darling? Keeping yourself for the one and only?' He came very close indeed and she didn't back away as she knew she would have done before. 'Hmm,' he said, 'not *quite* so untouched as I remember. Do I understand that that Spanish knight in shining armour has been staking a claim?'

Megan blushed. 'He's very particular,' she said.

Tony's eyebrows shot up in a droll look of enquiry. 'And you are not?'

'I don't understand Spanish customs very well. I keep on doing the wrong thing. The girls here are so restricted and protected. I think, in their eyes, I'm the next best thing to being a scarlet woman!'

Tony's laughter was oddly comforting. 'If they think that about a little puritan like you, they must be strait-laced! Poor poppet, knowing you, I don't suppose you're even enjoying shocking them all!'

'No, I'm not!'

His laughter rang out again. 'I thought not! Poor, poor Megan!'

'Yes, well—' Megan began uncomfortably. She was rescued from having to say any more by the sudden activity of everyone around her. 'It looks as though we're going in to eat,' she went on with relief.

'Are you going to sit next to me?' he pleaded.

'I don't know. I'm here with a friend.' She looked about her vainly for Inez, wondering where the Spanish girl could have got to.

'If he brings you here, he can't be totally without any life,' Tony teased her.

'It isn't a he,' Megan told him, searching the crowd with her eyes. What a lot of people there were, crowding into the courtyard, all of them intent on enjoying themselves. There were quite a few girls in trouser suits, she noticed, and very nice they looked in them too! She was glad that she didn't have to be snobbish about tourists and what they chose to wear. Why, she thought, in future if she wanted to wear trousers, *any* trousers, she would do so, and the Valloris would just have to put up with it!

She spotted Inez standing in the shadows by the wall

and knew that she was afraid of being recognised. Megan beckoned to her and introduced her quickly to Tony. Inez stood, as stiff as a poker, and extended her hand, not quite looking at Tony.

'I have heard about you,' she said. 'You are one of Megan's friends, aren't you?'

'I hope so,' Tony answered, sounding so sincere that Megan suspected he was trying not to laugh. 'I hope to be a friend of yours too!'

'But that wouldn't do at all!' Inez told him. 'My friends are all very respectable. Megan is the only person I know who has men friends. My parents would not approve of my knowing you and—neither would Carlos!'

'Am I so terrible?' Tony asked her, laughing.

'But of course you are!' Inez's eyes fell demurely. 'I have heard all about the way you kissed Megan—'

'Really?' Tony said dryly. 'Megan should learn to keep her mouth shut!'

Inez smoothed down her skirt with a fragile hand. 'Why?'

'Because I don't come out of the incident very well,' he answered promptly. 'Are you two ladies going to allow me to escort you in to dinner?'

'Please,' said Inez, all her doubts gone. 'If we go in with all the others, Señor Valdez will not notice me.' She lowered her tone to a confidential whisper. 'I prefer that my family do not know that I have come here!'

'Very understandable,' Tony assured her. 'A pretty girl like you needs all the protection she can get against eager fellows like myself!'

Inez burst into ready laughter. 'You should not say such things!'

'You should not be so pretty and then I wouldn't!' he retorted.

Well pleased, Inez led the way into the old stables where the tables were laid out for the feast. There were tiny baked potatoes, bowls of salad, great, thick slices of bread, and a bottle of wine between every four people. As soon as they were seated, the barbecued chickens were brought and served, piping hot, by waiters dressed in traditional Mallorquin costume, as dexterous as they were handsome.

A group of young Spaniards went from table to table singing the songs of Majorca, songs that were softer and more tuneful than the better known flamenco songs of the mainland, but which nevertheless had the same distinctive Arab intonation. They asked for requests from the visitors and sang a song or two in English, with more gusto than accuracy. Megan enjoyed their efforts, however, and clapped as loudly as everyone else as they disappeared into another room where yet more tables were laid out.

'Have some more wine, Megan?' Tony offered, scarcely taking his eyes off Inez's vivid features. ' If you're going to sing with us later on, you'll need to keep your strength up!'

'No, no!' Inez interrupted. 'The *sangria* was stronger than you suppose. You must be careful! If you are not accustomed to drinking much, it is easy to take more than one means to!'

'I'll be careful,' Megan said thoughtfully. She sat back in her chair and watched Tony and Inez talking to each other, so interested in what they were saying that the rest of the world might well have not existed for them.

Carlos wouldn't approve, she thought. Inez had no experience of choosing her own friends, and Tony was certainly not the sort of friend her family would have chosen for her. It was a pity that they had run into him so early in the evening. It would have been better if they had met later, when Tony was safely mounted on a platform, well away from the dancers, and then Inez would not have needed to have spoken to him at all.

'Am I going to sing for you, Tony?' she asked suddenly.

His eyes met hers briefly. 'Isn't that why you came?'

She nodded uncomfortably. 'I suppose so. Inez wanted to come.'

Tony laughed easily. 'Of course she did! She had more sense than to tell her family where she is, which is more than I can say for a certain other young lady!'

Megan blushed. 'My parents came to hear me sing,' she said, stung.

'And the Spaniard too?'

'*Carlos?*' Inez breathed, much excited.

'Is that his name?' Tony drawled indifferently.

'No,' Megan answered evenly, 'Carlos was only walking along the street, if you remember? That was no doing of mine!'

Tony felt his jaw reflectively. 'I haven't felt the same since,' he said. 'What business was it of his?'

'Everything is Carlos' business,' Inez assured him. 'He is a very good friend of my family—'

'Inez is going to marry him!' Megan put in.

Tony gave her an interested look. 'And how do you feel about that?' he asked quietly. 'Having your knight in shining armour snatched from under your nose?'

'I don't like him,' Megan stated.

Inez was plainly shocked. 'Why not, Megan? Is it because he brought you to Mallorca against your will?'

Megan refused to answer. 'Let's not talk about him!' she said instead. 'I feel as if he's going to walk in on us at any moment as it is—'

'And you feel guilty about that?' Tony suggested.

'Only about Inez,' Megan said firmly.

Inez looked decidedly ruffled. 'But you can see that I am quite all right!' she told Megan indignantly. 'Now that we have a man to escort us, what is wrong with our coming here?'

117

Tony's laughter took on an edge of anger. 'Such naïvety ill becomes the pair of you in such a place as this!'

Megan bit her lip. 'It looks innocent enough to me,' she said. 'Just a lot of nice people enjoying themselves.'

'And you think that is how your Spaniard would see it?' he shot at her.

'He isn't my Spaniard,' she prevaricated. 'If he's anyone's, he's Inez's.'

'Says you!' Tony scoffed.

'It is true,' Inez assured him. 'Carlos does not approve of Megan, because of what you and she did in London—'

'*What we did?*'

'In Spain,' Megan said in a funny, remote voice that she scarcely recognised as her own, 'women are like Caesar's wife—above suspicion, or beyond the pale!'

'Poor Megan!'

She smiled bitterly. 'Don't waste your sympathy. Twenty-four hours was enough to convince me that I should be bored stiff if I stayed here long!'

Tony stared down at his plate, separating the flesh of the chicken from the bone with elaborate care. 'Poor Megan,' he repeated.

'I don't know what you mean!' she said sharply.

He didn't bother to answer. Instead he replenished all their glasses with wine and turned his attention wholly on to Inez, leaving Megan free to talk to the others who were sitting at their table. There was a young couple, blatantly on honeymoon, who were busy feeding each other from a single plate, and an elderly woman who seemed to be on her own. Megan smiled tentatively at her and was rewarded by a neighing laugh.

'Are you at our hotel?' she asked Megan.

Megan shook her head. 'No, no, I don't think so.'

'Thought I hadn't seen you. Mind you, there are

so many of us that one can't get to know everyone, can one? I prefer to keep myself to myself at home, but it's different on holiday. Never thought I'd ever be sitting here, I can tell you! What are you doing in Majorca, dearie?' She pronounced Majorca with a strong, English ' j ' without any concession to how anyone else might pronounce it. Megan loved her for it. She was so relaxed and ordinary and unfussed by the strangeness of her surroundings. Megan doubted that she ever worried about anything.

' Are you enjoying your stay?' she asked her.

' Oh yes, it's been lovely! A real treat to come away like this and not have to worry about the next meal until it comes to the table. What about you?'

' I love the island,' Megan answered.

' Bits of it,' the old woman agreed. ' I liked the Caves. Real romantic, I call them! Have you been there?'

' No, I haven't,' Megan admitted.

' You should go there. The Cuevas de Drach, that's what they're called. Something to do with a dragon. Perhaps they're shaped like a dragon, or something like that. I got a booklet on them, I was so taken with them, but I haven't read it yet.' She laughed suddenly. ' Don't suppose I ever shall if the truth be known.' She pulled open her capacious handbag and rooted about inside it, turning over her travel documents, postcards by the dozen, and a collection of cosmetics, paper-handkerchiefs and the other assorted objects that women carry about with them. ' I have it here somewhere,' she insisted. ' I know I have!' With a triumphant flurry, she produced the small booklet and pushed it into Megan's reluctant hands. ' Take it, dear. It'll tell you all about it for when you go yourself. I've seen it for myself and I don't really want to know how they found it all and things like that. I just loved seeing it, though my, I was tired out after we'd walked through it all! I was that glad to sit down and see those little boats gliding around to the music. Ever so pretty it was!' She sighed gustily. 'There's no doubt about it, my dear, you must go and see them for yourself!'

'I will!' Megan said enthusiastically.

'That's right, dear. Give you a thrill, it will, to see that!'

Their conversation came to a forcible end as a middle-aged man, dressed in baggy striped trousers and a scarlet jacket, came into the old barn and began to play the Mallorquin version of the bagpipes. The weird noise filled the room, rising and dying away, as stirring to the blood as the pipes of Scotland, but just as inappropriate in a confined space. He walked about the barn, his cheeks scarlet with the heat and the exertion of blowing, his tunes roaring over the tables and echoing round the rafters.

When he had gone into the other room one could hear the silence, like something living and breathing. Then, all together, everyone drew breath and went on with their conversations in a burst of chatter.

'Oh, look,' said Inez, 'they're bringing in the roast sucking pig!'

The piles of plates, with their left-over chicken bones, were swiftly taken away and fresh plates, each with an enormous helping of pork on it, brought in their stead. Megan regarded it with some disfavour, feeling that she had already eaten enough, but she was amused by Inez's frank delight in the dish that had been set before her, attacking it with a gusto that she had not brought to the chicken, or even to the sublimely delicious little baked potatoes.

It was good. Very good. Salt and pepper had been rubbed hard into the surface of the meat, which had then been barbecued over charcoal. The result was tender and succulent.

'We ought to be making a move to the dance hall,' Tony said reluctantly. He patted his stomach, looking completely satisfied. 'At the moment I feel more like going to sleep than working!' His eyes swept over Megan's face. 'Are you still determined to sing for us?' he asked her.

She nodded briefly, finishing her meat in a hurry. Inez, however, made no move to hurry. 'I want to eat my orange first,' she insisted. 'They're grown here, did you know that? They taste much better when they have just been picked off the trees. You'll have to wait for me.'

'We can't,' Tony answered. 'We have to go—the boys will be waiting for us. Why don't you bring your orange with you?'

Inez made a face at him, her full lips pouting with dismay. 'I think you are very unkind to me,' she complained.

'Some of us have to earn a living,' Tony retorted.

'That is no excuse for being unkind,' she argued.

'I am not unkind! You can stay if you want and finish your orange, taking as long as you want to about it, but Megan and I have to go across to the hall *now*. We have to arrange what numbers we're going to do, for one thing, and for another, the boys will want to see her again. They were disappointed when they found out she'd left us.'

'*Espere un momento*,' Inez begged prettily. 'I am coming, Tony. I am coming quickly, only I can't get out!' She sounded pathetic and very anxious to please, smiling at the English tourists and apologising for disturbing them as she wriggled past them, clutching her oranges in her hands as though nothing would part her from them.

It had started to rain outside, a gentle spray of silver rain descended from the lowering black clouds that hung in the sky, hiding the moon and the stars. A distant roll of thunder echoed round the hills and the accompanying lightning lit up the surrounding almond orchards in a bright white light, highlighting the fragile tracery of the ghostly blossom.

'Oh, I have no coat! I shall get wet!' Inez complained.

'We'll have to run for it!' said Megan, determined to be cheerful at all costs. She wanted this evening to be over—nothing more than that.

'Come, the quickest way is through the courtyard and round the back!' Tony instructed them. He took both girls by the hand and hurried them out into the rain towards the newly built dancing hall in the distance.

They arrived in a flurry of laughter, shaking the damp off their clothes and out of their hair. The hall was empty as yet, an enormous building built of brick, with high wooden rafters hung about with old-fashioned farming objects to give an illusion of age and authenticity. Down one side there was a bar, waiting to supply the dancers with refreshments during the next couple of hours. At one end was a high platform, the enormous amplifiers standing on each other at either side, completely dwarfing the space in the middle. Megan's lips twisted at the sight of them. It was obvious that it was the beat that was wanted here, not the gentle, subtle rhythms of the songs that she sang best.

'Well, darling, how do you like it?' Tony asked her.

Megan was conscious of Inez's curious eyes, resenting the endearment and yet excited by it. The Spanish girl was clearly expecting Megan to respond in kind, but Megan felt only sad and tired. She wished she hadn't come. *She didn't want to sing.* That was the truth of the matter, and that was the worst thing of all. There had never been a time in her whole life when she hadn't wanted to sing and hear the applause of an audience, and sing again. And now, quite suddenly, she was revolted by the whole idea of it. No, she thought, trying hard to be fair, it was not the singing in itself, it was the simple fact that she knew that

Carlos wouldn't approve. Botheration take Carlos!
She'd sing whenever she wanted to sing, and he could
like it or lump it! It was silly to quiver inside whenever she thought of him. He never would approve of
her, no matter what she did, so she might just as well
please herself.

This conclusion did little to fortify her resolve, however, as she mounted the steps on to the platform and
looked out across the large hall. Tables and chairs
were placed in groups all round the dancing space,
empty from the moment, but already peopled in her
imagination with hostile stooges of Carlos, brought
there by him, all of them waiting for her to make a
fool of herself.

'It's better than the Witch's Cauldron!' Tony said,
well satisfied. 'And the people are easily pleased.
You'll knock them out, my love! I'm quite jealous at
the thought of your success!'

'I don't want to sing!' Megan said through dry lips.

Tony looked at her in astonishment. 'Don't be
silly, love,' he advised.

'You don't understand—' she began.

But he cut her off with an angry look. 'It's you
who doesn't understand,' he said with a touch of
menace. 'We're making out here, no more than that.
If you don't sing with us, we'll go back to England as
second rate in everybody's opinion as when we came!
We need a good vocalist to show just how good we are,
and that vocalist is going to be you. It was fate that
made you come to this barbecue, my pet, and it's fate
that you're going to sing with us tonight. You walked
out on me once before and you're not going to do it
again. Is that understood?'

Megan winced. 'I've said I will sing, haven't I?'
she said proudly. 'But I don't want to!'

'Who cares what you want?' Tony exclaimed.

The rest of the band came into the hall at that
moment and their delight at seeing Megan did some-

thing to assuage the tumult of emotions within her. She shook hands with them, touched by their open delight that she should be singing with them again.

'We've needed you, Megan Meredith,' said one long-haired young man. 'Did Tony tell you?'

'I suppose he did,' Megan admitted.

'Well, I'm telling you! We wouldn't be here if we were on the up and up, now would we?'

Megan looked concerned. 'But surely, I thought it was a step up for you to be here?'

The young man shook his head, plunking a note or two out of his guitar. 'Who is going to discover us here?'

'Anybody could!' Megan insisted. 'Look at all the people who come here for their holidays. Some of them must be in the music business.'

'We're not *that* good. It's as simple as that. When you get up on to that platform, you watch the atmosphere change. They really listen to you, honey. We're merely noises off!'

Even so, Megan found it hard to believe him. She looked round to see where Inez was and saw that the Spanish girl had seated herself at one of the far tables in the hall with Tony in close attendance. Megan hoped that she wouldn't find Tony too attractive, as he could be when he wanted to be, for she didn't trust Tony not to try for a quick kiss, and that, she thought, would be the next best thing to a total disaster!

Then suddenly the doors were opened and the people came flooding into the hall, their coats hitched over their shoulders, and their evening sandals wet from the unexpected puddles outside. The women exclaimed shrilly, gasping with horror at the drenched hems of their long skirts; the men, in lower key, grumbled good-naturedly as the thunder rumbled overhead, finding themselves a table and settling their parties in congenial groups.

Tony came up to the platform, swinging himself up

on to it with a single athletic stride.

'Good evening, ladies and gentlemen! Does any-one here not understand English? No? Good! Then we can get going with the old favourites and get into the swing of things. We have a surprise for you tonight. Have I caught your interest? Well, she'll catch your hearts, ladies and gentlemen, in a special appearance, by very special request—Miss Megan Meredith!'

Short, sporadic applause greeted the announcement. Megan frowned at him. She knew that many of the people there thought that they ought to have heard of her and were applauding accordingly. It was a con-fidence trick, Megan thought indignantly. She would have preferred the applause to have come after she had sung, when she had earned it, but Tony only winked at her, grasped her hand and pulled her to the edge of the platform.

'What are you going to sing?' he asked in an undertone.

Megan swallowed. What was she going to sing? She couldn't think of a single song. Worse still, the faces upturned to look at her dissolved into blobs, and all of them looked angry, annoyed at being kept wait-ing when they had come there to dance. Tony's grip on her wrist tightened. 'Hurry up!' he warned her.

Megan tried to pull herself together. 'They want to dance,' she whispered back.

'They won't. Not once you open your mouth!| What are you going to sing, Megan?'

She swallowed again. 'I'd like to sing a traditional song,' she heard herself say in a quietly confident voice that was so foreign to her actual feelings as to be ridiculous. 'Perhaps you know it. It's an old Scottish, or some say Irish, air, called " I know where I'm going ".'

The desultory applause came again, stiffening Megan's pride in her own ability. She nodded to the band and waited, almost placidly, while they began to play, lost the melody and found it again. Then, at exactly the right moment, she opened her mouth and began to sing, holding the microphone very close to her lips so that her quiet, intimate style would be heard right at the back of the hall.

The lilting sound rose and fell until all else had fallen away. The band behind her had gained confidence now and they made fewer mistakes, not that anyone there cared much whether they played or not. They were carried away by the soft, liquid notes of Megan's voice that suited the music exactly.

> *I know where I'm going,*
> *And I know who's going with me,*
> *I know who I love—*
> *But the dear knows who I'll marry.'*

Her voice died away and there was complete silence in the hall for a long, devastating second, and then the applause came thundering, bringing the colour into her cheeks and a pleasurable light into her eyes.

'What did I tell you?' Tony whispered triumphantly. 'We'll get them dancing now! Mustn't give them too much of a good thing! We'll wait for them to ask for you again.'

Megan nodded quietly. She went to the side of the platform and waited for the band to break into a modern dance rhythm that crashed resoundingly about her and then slipped anonymously into the crowd below. Inez was still sitting at the same table at the far end of the hall and Megan hurried across to join her. But Inez was no longer alone. Megan came to a full stop several feet away from the table, wondering how best she could escape, but she was already too late. Carlos looked up and saw her and rose leisurely to his feet.

'Won't you join us?' he said pleasantly enough.

Completely tongue-tied, Megan sat as quickly as she

could in the chair that was the furthest away from him.

'Carlos heard you sing,' said Inez.

Megan's eyes widened. She cast a quick look at Carlos, to find him studying her thoughtfully, and she could feel the hot, uncomfortable colour sliding up her cheeks.

'You look guilty,' he observed. 'I wonder why?'

Megan had no intention of telling him. She wished that her heart wouldn't beat faster every time she set eyes on him, giving her a breathless feeling of frustration that she could very well do without. When he was out of sight, she was able to forget how attractive he was to her. It was unkind, she thought, that he should have such an effect on her, when he apparently had no effect on him whatsoever.

'What are you doing here?' she demanded, at her most unwelcoming. She knew that she sounded childish and tears of chagrin flooded into her eyes. She didn't want him to think of her as young and brash, or, worse still, *gauche*. She wished urgently that she was stunningly beautiful and as sophisticated as any of the other women he knew and admired.

His eyes scarcely blinked as he regarded her. 'I heard you were here,' he answered quietly.

'But who could have told you?' Inez put in. She put out a possessive hand and stroked the sleeve of Carlos' coat. 'Surely you were not worried about us?'

Carlos shrugged her away. 'About you? Certainly not.'

Inez pouted, looking so completely crestfallen that Megan would have laughed, if she had not been so frightened at the same time.

'You'd better get your coats,' Carlos went on. 'I am taking you both home.'

'Thank you,' said Megan, 'but I've agreed to sing again. Tony—'

'Ah yes, *Tony*! I thought you might find out that

he was here and that you wouldn't be able to resist seeing him again. How much is he paying you, Megan?'

'Paying me?' she asked, puzzled. 'I—I don't think he is,' she stammered.

'Then you are singing for him for love?' he suggested.

She stared at him, stricken. 'Margot told you!' she said.

'Yes,' he agreed unpleasantly, 'Margot told me, as you might have known that she would. Get your coat, Megan, you're going home. And don't argue any more! *Dios mio!* Do you think my patience is inexhaustible?'

Megan stood up unsteadily. 'I'm not going with you,' she said. 'I can't! I promised—'

'Then it looks as if you will find yourself forsworn, doesn't it?'

She might have argued further, even then, but the gleam of sudden amusement in his eyes prevented her. Her heart hammered against her ribs and she was afraid that he would guess at her feelings if she stayed there another moment. Without a word, she picked up her coat and rested it on her shoulders, following him meekly across the hall and out into the damp night.

CHAPTER IX

It had stopped raining, but the floodlighting picked
out the moisture in the drive, making it glisten like
diamonds in amongst the pebbles. Megan tried to pretend to herself that she was not nervous and that she
had only given in to Carlos because of Inez. If it
wasn't quite true, it helped her to think that it was,
and she was smiling as they approached Carlos' car.

'You will come with me, Inez,' Carlos directed, his
voice stern and hard. 'Megan will have to drive
Margot's car home.'

'Oh, but—' Megan protested.

Carlos glared at her. 'The traffic will not be so
heavy now. It is your own fault, however. I told you
not to drive the car until I have seen how well you
drive!'

'I drive very adequately,' Megan retorted.

'Yes, she does, she does,' Inez put in, licking her lips
with sheer nervousness as Carlos' uncompromising
expression was shown up by a nearby light.

'She had better,' he said. 'You may go first, Megan,
leading the way, and I shall follow. I shall be watching you the whole way.'

Megan's heart sank. 'Couldn't Inez come with me?'

'No, she will be safer with me.'

He was as good as his word. He held the door of
the tiny Seat open for her and shut it firmly on her
as soon as she had got in. Megan took a deep breath,
bitterly aware that her hands were trembling. Why
did he have to be so unkind? Why shouldn't she sing
if she wanted to?

She tried to start the engine without turning the
ignition key. She didn't dare look at Carlos. The
engine started at a touch once she had turned the key,
but she stalled it by letting in the clutch with a jerk

that she had never done before, at least not since the very earliest days of her driving lessons. It was *his* fault! She clenched her jaw and started the engine again. She felt sick with nerves, and that was his fault too!

Carlos wrenched open the door again, his eyes glittering in the beam from the floodlighting.

'Get out,' he said briefly.

Megan was not Welsh for nothing. In complete silence she pulled the door shut again, let in the clutch and drove off without a backward look. Sheer fury made her blind to everything else but the one object of wiping that superior expression off Carlos' face. If he thought she couldn't drive, she would show him that she could—that she could drive *magnificently!*

She barely hesitated at the entrance, turning into the road with a panache that made her hope he was close enough behind to see. She even remembered to stay on the right-hand side of the road, pushing the little car into a speed that made the bodywork rattle. A bicycle, without any lights, appeared suddenly in front of her, and she was obliged to swerve to avoid it. Its closeness to her wheels made her gasp and slow down a little. Some of her anger left her, allowing the nervous fright that Carlos inspired in her to reassert itself. She took a deep breath and tried to concentrate on what she was doing, but, at that moment, Carlos' car flashed past her and drew in in front of her, making it impossible for her to go on. She came to a reluctant stop and braced herself to meet his anger.

He got out of his car almost languidly. Megan had a horrid feeling that she was going to cry, but she bit her lip until it hurt, and waited. He stood for a long moment, looking down at her.

'Well, go on, say it!' she dared him, breaking the unbearable silence.

'I think from here it would be better if you were to follow me,' he said quite gently.

' I won't!' she snapped.

He raised his eyebrows. ' Just as you like, but you can scarcely sit by the side of the road all night.'

' I shall go back to the farmhouse!' she threatened.

He shrugged his shoulders. ' At least, this time, you will not have Inez with you!'

The tears gushed into Megan's eyes, blinding her for a moment. ' That's all you care about, isn't it? Well, let me tell you, Inez would have been quite all right with me! I know what she means to you! I would have looked after her!'

' I know you would, if you could,' he said.

Megan stared at him, forgetting that she hadn't wanted him to see her tears.

' I wasn't doing any harm. The band isn't anything if I don't sing with them. I thought I owed them that much.'

' We'll talk about it later,' Carlos answered. He sounded quite kind and that upset Megan more than ever.

' I don't think I can see to drive!' she complained, and sniffed.

Silently, he took a handkerchief out of his pocket and handed it to her. She blew her nose violently. ' Doesn't Inez drive?' she asked.

' No.'

' Doesn't she do *anything*?'

He smiled slowly. ' She expects to have a man around her to do it for her most of the time.'

' How—how restful!' Megan said nastily.

' You would do well to learn from her,' he answered sternly. ' She doesn't rush from scrape to scrape, getting herself talked about.'

' How dull!' Megan objected, but his words hurt all the same. ' She is older than I am,' she excused herself.

' Is she?' He sounded surprised. He was silent for a moment. ' Feel better?' he asked her. She nodded bleakly. 'And you will follow me to Palma?' Again she nodded. If she did go back to the farmhouse, she thought, she would only have to explain her absence to Tony, and that was impossible. He wouldn't understand any more than she did. Live your own life, pet, he would say, and he would be right. Only how did one live one's own life when faced with the whole weight of Carlos' disapproval? That might not matter to Tony, but it mattered to her! It mattered to her more than she would have believed possible.

'*Muy bien,*' Carlos rapped out, making her jump. 'I shall take you to the Calle Morey first. You can be putting the car away while I take Inez home.'

'I should have thought you'd do that for me!' Megan sighed.

He laughed suddenly. 'Another time,' he said. 'This time it is important to get you home as quickly as possible.'

'Why?' she asked.

His laughter vanished. 'I prefer not to have either you or Inez discussed by my stepmother and her friends.'

'No,' Megan admitted sadly. 'She is no friend of mine, or she wouldn't have told you where I was going tonight.'

Carlos jerked himself upright. 'Don't hold that against her, *pequeña.* I would have found you anyway.'

He went back to his own car, swinging it easily back on to the road, travelling at a sober pace along the road to Palma. Megan followed, glad of the red lights ahead of her, guiding her through first the suburbs and then the complicated, cobbled streets of Palma.

When they approached the place where the Valloris parked their cars, he flashed his lights and drove away with Inez, leaving her to put Margot's car away and to go back to the house by herself. She did so quickly, hoping to get into the house and escape to her room before Margot realised that she was back. She was not, she told herself, ready to see Margot yet. Her anger with Carlos had died in her need to please him, but her anger with his stepmother still burned within her, for there was one thing she simply couldn't understand. If Margot had not wished them to go to the barbecue, why hadn't she said so? Why had she encouraged them to go and then told tales behind their backs?

The house was in darkness. Megan didn't bother to turn on any of the lights, but crept up the stairs to her room, shutting the door with a little click behind her. The ornate bed looked immense in the shadowed darkness, shrouded in the curtains that fell from the coronet near the ceiling. Megan crossed over to it and switched on the bedside light. Immediately, the room was transformed, the shadows banished.

Megan flung herself full-length across the bed, turned slowly over on to her back and stared up at the gilt coronet and the ornate ceiling above it. Carlos, too, must have lain on this bed often, she thought. Probably he, too, had taken refuge here from his stepmother. She wondered what it was that he would say to her about her singing with the band. It ought to be easy to explain to him that the band would never get anywhere without her, that it was her singing that raised them out of the ordinary, and that to get discovered it was important that she should be heard with them. She would tell him about it tomorrow, she thought.

She wriggled her shoulders and began to sing to herself, crooning her way through several old Welsh songs that she had learned from her father as a child. It was then that she noticed a long, thin package on her pillow and she reached out for it, feeling it with her fingers to try to discover what it was. A card dangled from the pretty pink paper and she glanced at it, curious to know who could have put it on her pillow.

This was my mother's. I shall teach you to use it myself, so don't bother to ask Margot. Carlos.

Megan blinked at the card, excitement rising within her. She unwound the paper with elaborate care and revealed a silk fan, hand-painted and mounted on an ivory frame that clicked satisfactorily when the fan was opened or shut. She spread it carefully and gazed down at the painted silk. A great number of Spanish wild flowers were displayed, so beautifully that they might have been real had it not been that the years had added a certain dusty darkening to the paint. It was the most exquisite fan that Megan had ever seen —and Carlos had given it to her.

' I wish to see you in my study when you have finished your breakfast.'

Megan's eyes sought Carlos' to find them bleak and very dark. She hoped, without much conviction, that he wasn't going to be angry with her. She wanted to thank him for the fan and if he was still cross with her she wouldn't be able to. She had rehearsed exactly what she was going to say to him and she still felt her gratitude to be quite inadequate. If he began by bullying her, she wouldn't even be able to thank him with the carefully planned speech she had prepared for the occasion.

' Did you hear me, Megan?'

Margot looked up lazily. ' I wish you wouldn't be so autocratic so early in the morning,' she complained. ' And what do you want to see Megan about? She is my companion, and if anyone is going to speak to her about last night, it ought to be me, don't you think?'

' I didn't know you objected to my going,' Megan sighed. ' You didn't say anything when Inez asked you if we could go!' She bit her lip, aware that Carlos was watching her closely. She wished she hadn't mentioned Inez. She had to remember that he was in love with Inez and that eventually he would marry her.

'My dear,' Margot laughed, 'of course not! I quite thought that Inez's parents were going with you!'

Megan's eyes dropped. 'Does it matter?' she asked, tired of the whole affair.

'Not to me!' Margot assured her readily. 'I never wanted a companion in the first place. More nuisance than you're worth! Nothing personal, my dear, I assure you, but with two young daughters of my own, I feel I have enough on my hands without having to chaperone you as well!'

'I see,' Megan said stiffly.

'I'm sure you do,' Margot went on. 'Perhaps you ought to have a talk with Carlos.' Her eyes shone maliciously across the table as she studied her stepson's totally indifferent face. 'Perhaps you can find out why he brought you here?'

Megan subsided into an embarrassed silence. She couldn't bring herself to look at Carlos, but she could well imagine the rigid lines of his face. The silence built up while they all waited for Carlos to say something, anything, but he appeared not to have heard a single word his stepmother had said. He finished his breakfast with all of his normal unhurried indifference and then rose to his feet.

'Shall we say in ten minutes?' he said to Megan.

'Very well,' she said.

Margot watched Carlos leave the room and then she laughed. 'Poor Carlos! I fancy he bit off more than he can chew with you! I daresay Pilar helped him. She has always loved doing the opposite to pouring oil on troubled waters. I suppose she thought that he would find it amusing to have you here?'

Megan strove to make her voice sound quite normal as she answered. 'I don't think so. She thought Carlos would be in Barcelona. I think they were both worried in case you were lonely here by yourself. They thought you'd feel more at home with somebody English with you.'

'But Carlos is not in Barcelona,' Margot pointed out.

'No,' said Megan. 'He's overseeing your new bathroom.'

'You sound as if you resent his care for me,' Margot taunted her. 'I can see that you are in love with him, my dear, but I shouldn't let him see it if I were you. A man like Carlos is very easily bored, and you're not very old, are you?'

Megan said nothing. She felt humiliated that Margot should read her so easily and knew that if she knew her young companion to be in love with her stepson, then very likely Carlos knew it as well.

'If you will take my advice, you won't try and shift the blame on to Inez, or on to me. Carlos won't admire you for it, nor would he believe anything against Inez or any member of his family. He is like his father in that way, only more so, because his mother was stiff-necked and Spanish too.'

'I shall tell him I'm leaving,' Megan burst out.

'Do!' Margot invited her. 'I only wish he'd agree to your going!'

'He can't keep me here against my will!'

'Oh, surely not against your will?' Margot opened her eyes very wide. 'Shut the door as you go out, dear.'

Megan was shaking as she knocked on the door of Carlos' study. She put it off for as long as she could, wishing that she could think of some reason why she should escape from him and his household without another word being said.

'*Adelante!*'

Megan opened the door a crack, feeling more than a little foolish. The door was impatiently pulled out of her hand and she came face to face with Carlos.

'I—I'm sorry about last night,' she began at a gallop.

'Come in,' he invited. 'Sit down. I wish to talk to you.'

' Yes?'

He looked amused. ' It must be your guilty conscience that's giving you such a hangdog look.'

She eyed him gravely. ' Carlos, I must go back to England.'

' Running away?'

She nodded. ' I think I am,' she admitted. ' I think that's exactly what I'm doing.'

' May one ask why?'

She shook her head. ' I don't think so,' she said with a quaint dignity. ' Isn't it enough that your stepmother doesn't want, or need, a companion? She —she doesn't like me.'

If she had hoped that he would reassure her as to her popularity with his relations she was destined for disappointment.

' No,' he agreed, ' she doesn't.' He smiled at her. ' She doesn't like you at all. I wonder why not?'

' Oh, I can tell you that!' Megan said with a kind of harsh bitterness. ' She doesn't know what I'm doing here, and I don't either! You made her have me as a companion, and she doesn't know what to do with me. Why did you?'

Carlos sat down elegantly behind his desk. His dark green eyes looked her up and down, the intimacy of his expression making her blush a little.

' You're growing up,' he murmured.

Megan felt a sudden urge to stick out her tongue at him, to show him that she wasn't grown up at all, but she didn't do it. She sat down on the nearest chair, smoothing her skirts down over her knees, a hopeless task, for they were much too short, and pretended that she didn't know that Carlos was still watching her.

' Why did you?' she repeated.

He shrugged his shoulders. ' An impulse, I suppose.'

' An *impulse*? But you can't rearrange people's whole lives on impulse, c-can you?' She hoped she sounded indignant rather than hurt, for she was hurt, though she would have been a great deal more hurt if she had believed him, she reflected. She didn't relish being no more than a charitable impulse.

To her surprise, Carlos looked more amused than ever. 'Do I have to tell you?' he asked.

'Yes, I think you do.'

'Very well then.' He tipped his chair back, his expression mocking. 'I was overcome by jealousy when I saw you in Tony's arms and I thought I'd make sure that he couldn't have you—'

'Until you'd looked me over and seen if you wanted me yourself?' she suggested, more than a little shocked.

'Something like that,' he said dryly.

'I don't believe a word of it!' she exclaimed. 'You'd never seen me before!'

'How do you know?'

She sat very still. 'Had you?'

'As a matter of fact I had. I had been in the Witch's Cauldron earlier and I heard you sing.'

'Oh,' she said.

'I saw you with your parents shortly after. It was easy to see that they were not exactly behind your career. I merely took advantage of that fact.'

'But why?'

'I had my reasons. I thought I was going to be in Barcelona for most of your stay here and I didn't want Margot turning my mother's house upside down because of an old resentment that she can't forget. I thought you had sufficient character to see that she didn't do that.'

'But *I* couldn't prevent her!'

'Not on your own, but I should have been behind you in the last resort. The house needs modernising, but not in Margot's way. I like what you did to the little sitting-room, for instance.'

Megan stared at him doubtfully. 'But you didn't know me *then*,' she insisted.

He smiled. ' I think I did '

' On the strength of a couple of songs?'

' A little more than that.'

She hesitated, trying to remember exactly what she had said to him that first, cold, snowy night. ' I can't think what.'

' Some day I'll tell you,' he teased her. ' When you're quite, quite grown up!'

' I'm grown up now,' she sighed. ' And I'm going back to England whatever you say. Carlos, I have to go!'

He frowned. ' Not quite yet,' he said. ' I have to go to Barcelona for a few days and I want you here while I'm gone. I'll bring Pilar back with me when I come. If you still want to, you can go back to England then.'

' Thank you,' she said simply.

The amusement came back into his eyes. ' You may not want to go,' he warned her.

' I think I shall. Nobody really wants me here, not your stepmother, nor Inez, nor—'

' Has Inez been unkind to you?' he demanded.

' No, of course not,' she denied uncomfortably. ' But she can't understand why you brought me here either. I must say, I don't think it was very kind of you, Carlos, to tell her how we met! You might have known what she would think!'

The amusement left his face, leaving it stern and withdrawn. ' And what does she think?' There was a dangerous edge to his voice that made Megan blink. She cast him a quick look of disapproval, wondering that he should ask. What should his fiancée think under the circumstances?

' I think she would prefer to be the centre of your attention. You're not very attentive, are you?'

' Is there any reason why I should be?'

Her eyes widened. ' I don't believe you care about her—about *anyone*—as a person in their own right! We're all puppets for you to manipulate to suit your own convenience! I'm thankful that I shall never marry a Spaniard! I think you're all hateful! You expect every woman to hang on your every word and you don't care about them at all! All you want is to amuse yourself with them and for them to be there when you want them, but you don't care a rap for their feelings!'

He laughed. 'I have to confess that I have not interested myself much in Inez's thoughts and feelings,' he admitted, completely unrepentant.

'It's nothing to be proud of!' she reproved him fiercely.

His eyebrows rose haughtily. 'Indeed?'

'You don't know what loving anyone means!' Megan went on, thoroughly ruffled.

'Is that so?' he drawled. 'Do you?'

Megan gave him an outraged look. She would have flung herself headlong into further speech, but something in his expression prevented her. 'N-no,' she admitted. 'At least—'

'Yes?' he prompted her.

She chewed on her lip resentfully. 'That is,' she amended, 'I do know what loving someone means, only I've never been in love with anyone.'

'There is a difference,' he agreed. 'I have been in love often and often, but loving someone is something else again. I think I have only loved my mother.'

Megan took a deep breath. 'Don't you love Inez?' she burst out.

'No,' he said.

She turned this over in her mind, feeling sorry for the Spanish girl and, in a way, for Carlos himself. 'I think you love Pilar,' she said at last. 'She wouldn't have such an affection for you if you didn't.'

His expression softened. 'Yes,' he agreed, 'I am fond of both my sisters.'

Megan twisted her fingers together thoughtfully. 'Haven't you any particular affection for Inez?'

'Should I have?' he retorted.

She nodded quickly. 'I don't know what you mean by loving,' she told him abruptly. 'You said your wife would be loved as the mother of your children, but won't she want to be loved for herself?'

'Would you?' he enquired.

She nodded again.

'Then you probably will be,' he said. The warmth of his voice made her heart beat in an unfamiliar and unwelcome way.

'I'd hate to be chosen for—for my pedigree and general suitability!' She wondered why he laughed, but she didn't dare look at him in case that certain look was back in his eyes. 'Don't you want your wife to love you at all?' she ended, her voice breaking.

'I intend that she shall love me.' He stood up, coming round the desk towards her. 'She shall love me devotedly and without reservation—'

'But you won't love her!' Megan protested.

'I haven't said that. There are many kinds of love. I have told you that my wife will not go unloved.' He put out his hands to her, but she couldn't bring herself to put her own hands in his and put them instead behind her back, like a child. 'Nor will I choose her for her pedigree,' he promised. 'My own pedigree will have to do for both of us!'

Megan turned her back on him. 'What else did you want to say to me? I thought you were still angry about last night?'

'So I am!'

She turned back to face him, her face anxious. 'Because of Inez? But truly she came to no harm—'

'No, not because of Inez!'

She thought about this for a moment. 'Then why are you angry?' she asked.

'I had hoped that you would see this Tony of yours for what he is, that you would have grown up that much while you have been here. But what do I find? That you have learned nothing! That you are happy to sing for him again, whenever he lifts his little finger! And I wonder why he has your loyalty, when he has done little to earn it, and then I think you must be a little bit in love with him, no?'

'No,' she said. 'You don't understand!'

'No, I don't!'

'I *like* singing,' she said in a curious. flat voice. 'One day I shall sing again. I have to earn my own living. I'm not like your Spanish girls who expect to be supported by their families until they marry. I have to support myself!'

'By allowing this Tony to support you?'

She shook her head. 'By singing,' she said.

'Very well,' he answered distantly. 'But I will ask you not to sing again in public while you are under my roof. When you go back to England you may please yourself. Here, you are in my charge, and I will not have you performing in public. Is that clear?'

'Yes,' Megan managed.

She raised her eyes to him and saw that he was looking positively cheerful, as well as being quite unaccountably pleased with himself. How could he, when she felt more miserable than she ever had in her whole life?

'I'll be back from Barcelona at the end of the week. Look after yourself until then,' he said gently. 'I have to go to Barcelona or—I'll tell you about that when I get back!'

She went to the door and opened it reluctantly. She wished that he had, at least, touched her, given her something to live on while he was away. But then why should he? She had no claim on him. Oh dear, she thought, the sooner she went back to England and never saw him again the better! Then with a sudden, devastating sense of relief she remembered the fan he had given her. She turned back to him, her whole face alight with pleasure.

'I meant to thank you first of all for the fan,' she

told him. 'I shall treasure it always. I'm very proud to have something of your mother's. I would have thanked you before, only I knew you were angry with me for—for last night. But I want you to know that you couldn't have given me anything better—' She broke off, afraid of what she might say. 'Thank you very much,' she ended abruptly.

'When I come back I shall teach you how to use it,' he promised.

She shook her head, her eyes blinded by tears. 'When you come back, I shall go home to England,' she reiterated.

'Perhaps, for a little while,' he agreed. 'But, Megan, be careful while I'm away. Margot will do nothing to protect you because—because of something that happened between us long ago. It's important to me that the people here should think well of you, as important as if you were Pilar or Isabel. Will you remember that?'

'I'll try to do what you would wish,' she promised, though why it should matter to him what people should think of her was beyond her.

'Will you?' he drawled, his smile twisted. 'You won't see Tony while the dragon is safely away?'

She smiled herself, amused by the idea. 'No,' she said.

'If you do, I shall undoubtedly be told about it!' he warned her bleakly.

'But I won't!' she protested. She felt suddenly happy and hopeful that perhaps everything would turn out all right after all. 'Carlos, look after yourself in Barcelona too, won't you?'

His look of surprise rewarded her. 'I shall be too busy to get into much trouble,' he assured her dryly. '*Hasta luego, amada!*' He leaned forward and kissed her fleetingly on the mouth. 'Is that better, *hija*?'

Megan gave him a mischievous smile, her spirits completely recovered. 'Much better!' she said.

143

CHAPTER X

Time without Carlos went slowly. Megan, who had never been lonely before, was surprised to discover that she was lonely now. There was nothing for her to do. Indeed, she only saw Margot at mealtimes, and she suspected that Inez was avoiding her, probably because she had got into trouble with her family for going to the barbecue with only an English girl as chaperone.

Megan spent the first day writing to her family, preparing them for her imminent return to England. This was a harder task than she had expected, for she had the feeling that they wouldn't be very pleased to see her back and as anxious to go on with her singing career as ever. What was so bad about wanting to sing? she asked herself. There were worse ways of earning a living. Why, oh, why was it so hard to persuade them of that?

She and Margot had their evening meal together in the sitting-room.

' It's too much trouble to set the table in the dining-room for a couple of women,' Margot said sweetly. ' The maids have enough to do, don't you think?'

Megan wasn't sure that she agreed with her, but she only nodded and meekly sat down, searching for some topic of conversation that would interest the older woman.

' Carlos says he is bringing Pilar back with him,' she said. ' It will be lovely to see her again.'

Margot smiled with a touch of malice. ' I suppose Inez has been forbidden your company? Such a pity! Mallorca hasn't been the answer to your dreams after all, has it, my dear? It was very naughty of Carlos to have brought you here.'

Megan looked at her under the cover of her eyelashes. Margot was looking pleased about something, she thought, and she wondered what it could be that had given her so much pleasure.

'I expect he thought you would like someone English with you,' Megan remarked. 'He tries to make things easier for you—'

'Like disappearing the moment the builders arrive to do the bathroom?' Margot cut in. 'The noise has been terrible all day!'

Megan was startled. 'I haven't heard them!' she exclaimed.

'You wouldn't! You're on the other side of the house. I told Carlos it was quite ridiculous to give you that room—it's one of the biggest we have—but he insisted and, just like in everything else, he had to have his own way!'

'It is his house,' Megan reminded her gently.

Margot looked scornful. 'Don't be naïve, my dear. The house is as much his mother's now as it was when she was alive. That's why he made me come here. I know it!'

'But why?'

Margot smiled bitterly. 'Because he hates me!'

'Oh, surely not!'

'Does that shock you? It used to shock me when he was just a little boy that the man I loved happened to have fathered before I had met him, but I've grown used to it over the years. I suppose he resented my taking his mother's place.'

'He may have done,' Megan agreed justly.

'He did! He was an impossible child! His mother's family was ready enough to dislike me and most of my husband's money came from them, so that was bad enough, but Carlos made sure that none of my children ever had a penny of that money. Everything, every last peseta, came to Carlos when my husband died.'

'Isn't that customary?' Megan enquired. 'I mean

Carlos is the eldest son.'

' As he is never tired of pointing out! No, it wasn't that that we quarrelled about. What he resented was his father falling in love with me. His own mother was not a very lovable woman—my husband married her largely because it was expected of him. It was a wretched marriage, as was to be expected. My husband often said that he had never known any happiness until he married me!'

Megan was saddened. She could imagine the young Carlos having to listen to such remarks and she felt sadder still.

' Carlos loved his mother,' she said.

' He romanticised her and her family encouraged him to remember her as somebody out of a fairy-tale, I regret to say.' Margot's expression grew more alert as a thought came to her and she turned it over in her mind, well pleased with it. ' I think I'll take you to meet them,' she said carefully. ' Better, we'll give a party and invite them to come What do you think?'

Megan wondered uncomfortably if Carlos would like his family to be entertained by his stepmother while he was away. Then she gave herself a mental shake, reflecting that she was being silly about nothing. Margot had been the Señora Vallori for many years now, and the first Señora Vallori's parents must have come to terms with the situation long before this.

' I am here to help you in any way I can,' Megan murmured out loud.

' So you are!' Margot remembered. ' Well, it seems that at last I have found something for you to do. I'd like you to drive me to Soller tomorrow. They have a small place there where they live some part of every year. Señora de la Navidades, Inez's mother, was telling me that she thought the old lady was in residence. She has an unmarried daughter who tags along with her, poor dear, and I suppose she will be there too.'

'Can't you telephone and find out?' Megan asked.

Margot gave a little gasp of laughter. 'The old lady had the telephone taken out,' she explained. 'She said it gave Carlos an excuse to be lazy and to give her a ring instead of going to visit her. Naturally she thought I was trying to keep him away from her.'

Megan was surprised by the naked dislike in the older woman's voice. 'Did you?' she asked. 'I mean, did you keep him away from his grandparents?'

'Grandmother. His grandfather had died long before I came on the scene. Well, yes, I suppose I did. He would have moved there entirely if I had allowed him to, but my husband wouldn't have liked that. He was very conscious that Carlos was his son and had to be brought up under his own roof. It wasn't my fault! I told Carlos that it angered his father when he spent so much time with his grandmother, but he wouldn't listen of course, just as he never listens now. He said his grandmother was lonely and had a right to his company. You wouldn't believe that any boy would think of such a thing, would you? But Carlos did. He went on and on about it and, in the end, I forbade him to visit her at all. He kept getting out though and one day I beat him for it. He didn't say a word. He broke the stick into tiny pieces and threw them at me. That was the end of any hope I had of making friends with him.'

'He must have been very fond of his grandmother,' commented Megan.

'Only because she disapproves of me! Margot frowned, her temper getting the better of her discretion. 'She would have done anything to have ruined my marriage! Señora Llobera has never had a good word to say for me! She made my life a misery when we came here. In the end I persuaded my husband to live permanently in Barcelona. I can't tell you what a relief it was to get away from her and her horrid cronies who are nearly as bad!' It will be interesting to see what she makes of you!'

Megan smiled lazily. 'I don't suppose she will approve of me either,' she said.

'Probably not,' Margot agreed promptly, looking pleased at the thought. 'I expect the Navidades will have told her all about your taking Inez to the barbecue and then leaving her on her own while you sang to the tourists. It's hardly the sort of incident that is calculated to gain her approval. But then it doesn't matter to you either way, does it?' She smiled brightly, watching Megan out of the corner of her eye.

'No,' Megan agreed. 'It doesn't matter to me.' But she wasn't above admitting to herself that she would like Carlos' grandmother to approve of her, and to like her a little, just as she would have liked Carlos' mother to have liked her had she been alive.

Margot sat in the passenger seat making critical remarks about Megan's driving, the state of the roads, and how trying the sun was when it was so low in the sky.

'I hate the winter,' she said. 'I hate having to wear a coat all the time. You'd think the climate here would allow one to go out without having to wear half one's wardrobe on one's back.'

'It was snowing in England,' Megan said dreamily. She guided the car carefully on to the road to Valldemosa, relaxing only when they had left Palma behind them and were passing through the first of the farms and the almond orchards, still white with delicate blossom. 'I thought they were exaggerating when they said come and see the blossom of a million almond trees in Majorca! It's so beautiful that it doesn't seem true!'

'It is pretty,' Margot dismissed it. 'Would you like to stop and see the convent where Chopin and George Sand stayed when they were here?'

Megan went pink with pleasure. 'Do you mean

it? You must have been there many times before! Are you sure it wouldn't bore you?'

'Not at all,' Margot said politely. 'Carlos will be pleased if he thinks I have been entertaining you properly.'

Megan laughed. 'I don't suppose he'll enquire,' she said.

Margot's eyes snapped with amusement. 'But you'd like him to? Don't worry, my dear, I'll make sure he knows about all your doings as soon as he gets back. I'll tell him how helpful you are being over my little party.'

Valldemosa was only seventeen kilometres from Palma. The road climbed up towards the picturesque village, the rose-coloured tiles rose steeply over gold-coloured walls, crowding into one another at different angles to one another, in a pleasing kind of chaos. The delicate almond blossom shone brightly in the sunshine and the green of the fields were bright with winter lushness. It must have been very much the same when George Sand had taken her sick lover there.

'Do you like Chopin's music?' Margot asked.

Megan nodded enthusiastically. 'It's funny to think that he composed his stuff here on a piano that was bady out of tune and had only been loaned to him while he waited for his own to get here from Paris. Then, when it did arrive, it was too late. He was leaving in a day or so.'

Margot looked bored. 'I shouldn't have thought he was your cup of tea. Don't you sing more popular stuff?'

'Mostly,' Megan admitted. 'One can like all sorts of things that one can't sing, though.'

'I suppose so,' Margot agreed. 'I didn't know about the piano.'

Megan turned into the main street of the little town and triumphantly parked the car. It was cold when they got out of the car, a wind blowing down the hills and along the street. Megan shivered and tied her coat tighter about her. The shops were not as exciting as she had expected. There were one or two Spanish bars, advertising themselves as English tea-shops, and several souvenir shops, all selling much the same goods. Margot strode past them all without a single glance to either side. Megan, who would have liked to have browsed through the carved wooden figures and the collections of Spanish hats and unlikely-looking dolls dressed in Mallorquin costumes, followed after her, wondering where they were going.

Margot knew exactly where she was going. She turned up a steep slope, pointing to the signpost that directed them to La Real Cartuja, the Royal Carthusian Monastery that was founded in 1339 by King Martin, who gave up the royal palace of the Kings of Majorca for the purpose. In 1853, the monks left the convent and it was used as a kind of hotel, to put up visitors who wanted to hire the three-roomed cells for their own use. It was in the winter of 1838–39 that George Sand, her son and daughter, and her lover, Frédéric Chopin, moved in and suffered the rigours of a totally unheated Mallorquin winter, in beautiful surroundings that were apparently hardly appreciated by any of them. Nevertheless, it was here that Chopin composed some of his most famous Preludes, while moving steadily nearer to his death. What kind of nurse George Sand made, in her male attire and busy writing her own brilliant account of their time there, is better left to the imagination. If she disliked the local inhabitants, there is no doubt that they found her, and her whole ménage, bizarre in the extreme.

Margot bought the tickets for them to enter and hurried Megan through the rooms that the famous visitors had occupied. Both pianos, the one Chopin had actually used and the one he had bought in Paris and had had transported at such cost, were proudly displayed, together with some of his music and the handwritten manuscript of George Sand's *Winter in Majorca*. But, if anything, Megan preferred the quaint little gardens that were attached to each cell, each one cut off from the others by high walls. From these one could see the most superb view, down from the little town and across the valley below, almost as far as Palma itself.

'They must have been happy here!' Megan exclaimed.

'If it was as cold then as it is now, I should think they were glad to get back to civilisation,' Margot retorted. 'I would never have agreed to come here in the first place. Romance, especially romantic surroundings, is seldom comfortable.'

Megan gurgled with laughter. 'Perhaps not. I wonder if the blossom was out while they were here?'

'I don't know,' Margot answered. 'Probably not.'

It was obvious that the older woman was glad to leave the atmosphere of the convent behind her. She refused to visit the private rooms of the old palace that had been left as they had been in the days when royalty had visited Valldemosa, and hurried Megan back to the car.

'It isn't far to Soller,' she said, 'but the road runs slap over those mountains and we won't be able to go very fast. Will you be all right driving, or shall I?'

Megan wondered which the other woman would prefer. 'I expect you know the road better than I do,' she began.

'That's why I'd prefer you to drive,' Margot said firmly. 'Carlos says you're quite a good driver.'

'Does he?' Megan was pleased beyond all reason. 'I don't know why he should think that,' she added. 'I haven't exactly shone on the occasions when he has seen me at the wheel.'

'Carlos always thinks he knows everything whether he does or not,' Margot remarked unkindly. 'If you can get us safely over those hills, I'll tell him what a good driver you really are!'

Megan was very much on her mettle as they climbed away from Valldemosa, taking the road to Soller. It was not particularly steep on the way up, but on the other side, they almost fell down the side of the cliff into the valley in which Soller was situated. Megan changed down into a lower gear, using the engine of the car to brake their descent, thus allowing her to be more sparing with her use of the protesting foot-brake.

' It's worse getting back,' Margot announced gloomily.

' It's a pity you haven't a more powerful car,' said Megan.

' Oh, you can't do better than these little Seats,' Margot affirmed. ' Old age is all that's wrong with this one. I bought her second-hand years ago. I *never* came to Mallorca in those days, so it didn't matter what sort of car I had here.'

Megan picked out the road to Soller, pausing at the crossroads to see if any traffic was going the other way.

' The house is at Puerto de Soller, not in the town itself,' Margot directed her. ' You have to turn left here.'

Megan did so and, a few minutes later, they came to a large, imposing house overlooking the sea. Two pillars marked the entrance, both of them bearing the Llobera crest, that Megan recognised from the one in Carlos' room in Palma. Without having to be told, she turned into the drive and parked the car beside a huge scarlet poinsettia that offered a certain amount of shade.

Margot looked about her with distaste. ' Osten-tatious, isn't it?' she said with displeasure.

Megan, who was busy admiring the sheer beauty of her surroundings, couldn't agree with her. If any-thing, the house was shabby and badly in need of a coat of paint. But nothing could hide the pleasing lines of the building, built to take the best advantage of the view of the sea and the harsh, stony mountains. And the garden was a delight, full of flowering shrubs, orange trees, and the ubiquitous almond trees trailing their clouds of glory against the bright blue of the winter sky.

A dog came running out of the house, longing to bark at them but obviously unsure as to whether it was expected of him. There followed, more slowly, an old lady, dressed totally in black and walking with the aid of a stout stick. Her skin had been burned brown and was as wrinkled as a nut; her eyes, jet-black and autocratic. There was something familiar in the way she held her head and in the aristocratic air that dominated her frail body. This, without a doubt, was Carlos' grandmother.

Margot advanced hurriedly towards the old lady. 'Señora,' she exclaimed, 'you are here! How fortunate, as we have come to invite you to a little party I am giving.'

The old lady almost smiled, but refrained from actually doing so. 'How kind,' she murmured. 'Is Carlos with you?'

'No, no, unfortunately he is in Barcelona.'

'Of course,' the old lady said. She turned away from Margot, devoting her whole attention to Megan who was standing hesitantly beside the car, waiting to be introduced. 'Is this the English girl I have been hearing about?'

Megan coloured defensively. 'It depends what you've heard,' she said. 'I am English, or rather I am Welsh.'

The old lady laughed, her shoulders shaking. 'I had not heard that,' she admitted. 'Strange, because I told Carlos to tell me all about you!'

'Have you seen Carlos recently?' Margot demanded.

'He came over to see me the other day,' the old lady replied dryly. 'Didn't he tell you?'

'No,' Margot said reluctantly. 'I didn't know you were in residence until Señora de la Navidades told me. I brought Megan over to meet you. We've been visiting the Cartejo at Valldemosa.'

The old lády's attention was instantly diverted. 'Megan,' she repeated. 'Is that some kind of pet name?'

Megan chuckled. 'No, it's a real name,' she said.

'You must come inside,' the old lady invited. 'We can talk in comfort in my sitting-room. My daughter will entertain you, Margot, in the garden, as I am sure you will prefer.' She tucked her free hand into Megan's and started back into the house. 'You are very young, *cara mia*. Very, very young. I hope my grandson is behaving himself and not expecting too much too quickly?'

Megan felt herself colouring again. 'I am here as Señora Vallori's companion,' she said.

The old lady looked amused. Really, she was very like her grandson! 'And how do you like your employer?' she asked.

Megan was caught completely off balance. 'I—I like her. Naturally,' she claimed.

'I have never liked her,' the old lady returned, completely unperturbed. 'She was a poor comedown for Stefano after my daughter.' Her jet-black eyes surveyed Megan placidly. 'You don't believe me?' she accused, the corners of her mouth twitching with amusement. 'You think I am prejudiced? So I am! But I am not a fool and I have lived a long time in this world. I know a thing or two!'

Megan grinned, 'I'm sure you do!'

Señora Llobera rapped her sharply over the knuckles. 'So you have a tongue in your head!'

Megan rubbed her knuckles ruefully. 'I'm afraid so. Because of it, I am almost permanently in disgrace! With *everybody*!' she added somewhat wildly.

'Meaning with my grandson?'

Megan blinked, forcing herself to meet the ironic gaze of the old lady. 'I suppose so,' she admitted with a sigh.

'Don't be in too much of a hurry,' Señora Llobera advised. She pushed open the door of a small sitting-room and sat heavily in the nearest chair, breathing hard. 'How tiresome it is to grow old!' she complained. 'It is I who should be in a hurry! It is my ambition to see my grandson settled in life before I die. It is not much to ask, but I ask it of the good God every day of my life—and see how he repays me! By making my body a misery to me while I wait!' She laughed shortly. 'What do you think of Inez de la Navidades?'

Megan looked down quickly, hiding her eyes from the Señora's shrewd gaze. 'I'm not the right person to ask,' she said carefully. 'She—she seems to have led a very secluded life.' She glanced up. 'From an English point of view,' she added.

The old lady grunted. 'You're right. She has no depths. She would bore Carlos in a few weeks, just as his father bored his mother!'

'Did he?' Megan gasped before she could prevent herself.

The old lady's eyes twinkled. 'It is not something I tell everyone, but it is no more than the truth. It is something that Carlos will never admit, but then I don't suppose he was old enough to understand these things. All he knew was that he had a mother who was often restless and always impatient of the life she was forced to lead, and for this he blamed his father. Margot was the right wife for Stefano, but Carlos could only resent her. She seemed small and narrow after his mother.'

'Did she seem like that to you too?'

'Perhaps. I was not judging the whole female sex by one woman.'

Megan blinked. 'Do you mean that Carlos expects

women to bore him?' she asked frankly.

'I am afraid he might,' his grandmother answered.
'Do you bore him?'

Megan chuckled again. 'No,' she said. 'I annoy
him too much to bore him! He disapproves of my
wanting to earn my living by singing. He thinks I'm
a child in need of both protection and discipline.'

Señora Llobera laughed heartily. 'How old are
you?'

'Eighteen.'

'A great age!' the old lady mocked.

'Old enough!' Megan claimed, throwing back her
head in an impatient gesture.

'You may very well be right,' the Señora agreed.
'Do you sing well?'

Megan considered the point carefully. 'Not well,'
she said. 'I put a song across well—'

The old lady looked puzzled. 'You must excuse
me,' she said, 'my English is not well enough to understand the difference. You have a good voice, yes?'

'No. I have an adequate voice.' Megan's face lit
with laughter. 'I am better seen than heard,' she
explained with a touch of embarrassment.

'Ah! Now I understand exactly! I should like to
hear you sing some time, *niña*. I think it would amuse
me very much!'

Megan looked down her nose, liking the Spanish
woman very much indeed. 'I'm sure it would, *señora*,'
she said politely. 'But I am accustomed to a less
critical audience than you would be.'

Señora Llobera tapped her stick against the marble
floor. 'Carlos would have done better to have brought
you here to be my companion,' she said finally. 'I
shall tell him so. And now, Meganita, we had better
go and find Margot and hear when she is expecting us
to dine with her. Usually, I prefer not to go out at
night these days, but I think for once I shall make an
exception.'

Megan smiled at her uncertainly. 'Why do you call me Meganita?' she asked.

The old lady stood up, wincing at the pain in her limbs. 'Because I am Spanish and nearly sixty years older than yourself,' she said. 'It is a compliment implying affection, as I suspect you already know!' She looked at Megan sharply. 'I suppose my grandson has called you that?'

Megan blushed. 'Once,' she admitted. 'Usually he is far too cross!'

'Poor Carlito!' the old lady murmured.

'He is *never* cross with Inez!' Megan went on.

The old lady shrugged, losing interest. 'Naturally not,' she said. '*Venga*, little one. I shall need your arm if I am to stagger out into the garden again!'

'I hope you didn't mind my leaving you to talk to the Señora by yourself,' Margot said, as they headed for the mountains and home. 'She obviously wanted you to herself and it doesn't do to cross her.'

Megan frowned at the road ahead. 'I like her,' she said.

'She has a certain magnificence,' Margot admitted. 'She scares me to death! What did she say to you?'

Megan was surprised by the frank curiosity in the other woman's voice. 'It must be lonely for her here, with only her daughter for company,' she side-stepped the question. 'I expect she used to entertain a lot.'

'When her husband was alive,' Margot confirmed. 'Did she talk to you about the old days?'

'Not really. She said she would like to hear me sing. I think Carlos must have told her—'

'She probably heard about the barbecue from the Navidades,' Margot cut in maliciously. She thought for a minute in silence. 'Does she really want to hear you sing? Then we must oblige her. I'm sure you wouldn't mind entertaining us when she comes to dinner, would you, my dear?'

'I don't know,' Megan said doubtfully. 'I don't play well enough to accompany myself.'

Margot smiled. 'That's easily arranged! I'll ask Señor de la Navidades to lend us Tony Starlight and his band. You'll feel quite at home with them!'

'Oh, but—' Megan began.

'Nobody could possibly object to your singing in a private house as a favour to me,' Margot reassured her. 'Don't give it another thought, my dear. I'll arrange everything! Why shouldn't we give the old lady some pleasure? As you were saying, she gets little enough these days!'

It sounded very reasonable, put like that, Megan had to admit, but she worried about it all the same, as she threw the little car round the blind bends in the road as they made their way up the face of the mountain. The tyres protested and the engine shuddered, threatening to stall, each time they encountered a patch in the road, steeper than the rest and crumbling at the edges. Sometimes, if a car was coming down the hill at the same time, it was as much as Megan could do to hold the car on the road. In many ways it was a frightening journey, and by the time they reached the top, she felt a nervous wreck.

The fact was that she didn't want to see Tony again. Megan jumped in her seat and tried to analyse why she should suddenly feel like that about someone as innocuous as Tony. She liked him well enough, but he was sure to behave as though she were his personal property, and for some reason, the thought of his doing so in Carlos' house distressed her. Then she remembered that by the time his grandmother came to dinner, Carlos would be home again and would make Tony behave himself. She breathed deeply, shedding all feeling of responsibility for the evening. If Carlos was there, everything would be all right.

The road flattened out over the top of the mountain and then, in a series of hectic curves, it fell away below them down to the flat plain that stretched across the island to Palma. There was nothing, no wall or barrier, to keep one on the narrow, crumbling corners, nothing but a sheer drop down to the next phase of the cleverly engineered road beneath.

They had almost reached the bottom, and the backs of Megan's hands were pricking with reaction after the drive, when Margot found her voice again. 'What a pity Carlos won't be here to act as host to his grandmother,' she said. 'Perhaps your Tony would care to take his place?'

The car swerved dangerously to the side of the road.

Margot laughed lightly. 'Don't you think Carlos would like it?' she went on, as smooth as a cat playing with a frightened mouse. 'Never mind, dear, he won't be there to know!'

CHAPTER XI

The old lady looked tired when she stepped out of the hired car that had brought her and her daughter to Palma. Megan was concerned by the frail look about her eyes and the weariness with which she forced her legs to take her up the marble staircase upstairs. Her daughter, however, looked quite unmoved. She was a tall, angular woman, with a rough way of speaking that hid a peculiar tenderness in her relations with other people.

'I am Tia Anita,' she said abruptly to Megan. 'Seeing that no one has taken the trouble to introduce us!'

Megan shook her hand politely. '*Me llamo* Megan Meredith,' she responded. '*Mucho gusto, señorita.*'

Carlos' aunt smiled briefly. 'My mother told me you didn't speak Spanish. I appreciate your greeting me in my own language. It is a courtesy one does not look for from the young.'

'Señora Llobera looks tired,' Megan interposed.

'She should never have come!' her daughter retorted. 'What possible interest can she have in visiting this house when Carlos is not here? It is years since either of us have been welcome visitors in any Vallori house!'

Megan was silent, suspecting that as far as Margot was concerned this was very likely true. 'I wish Carlos was here tonight,' she sighed as they gained the top of the stairs.

Señorita Anita paused fleetingly in front of her dead sister's portrait, her face clouded. 'Her son *should* be here!'

Justice forced Megan to admit that Margot made a more than able hostess, even without benefit of having a host to help *her*. She found Señora Llobera a comfortable chair and insisted that she had a short rest while the others went into the larger, more formal *salon* and were given a drink before their meal.

' I should like to have Meganita with me,' the old lady said, just as the door was being shut on her.

Margot hesitated. ' I had hoped she would help me in the other room,' she said, reasonably enough.

The old lady's lower lip jutted out stubbornly. ' I wish to talk to the girl!' she reiterated. ' She amuses me and I want to hear what she has been doing.'

' Oh, very well!' Margot agreed sharply. She called to Megan, giving her a meaning look. ' Don't tire her with endless chatter, my dear. We don't want her having to go home in the middle of the festivities, do we?'

The old lady snorted. ' Just as if I were two years old!' She patted the chair beside her, looking round the room with interest. ' Come and sit here. They've changed this room since I was last here.'

Megan coloured prettily. ' I did most of it,' she confided. ' Carlos said I could.' She pointed to the picture over the fireplace. ' He allowed me to move that in here too. It makes the room, don't you think?' She turned to the old lady, anxious for her approval. ' We—we thought the house spoke too much of his mother,' she confessed.

' Quite right!' Señora Llobera approved. ' She is no longer here to enjoy it. I am surprised Carlos agreed to the changes, though.'

' I don't think he minded. His own room is very comfortable,' Megan pointed out. ' I think he wanted to please Margot, because she doesn't really want to live here and he doesn't think she'll be happy on her own in England.'

The old lady's eyes glittered in the half-light from the lamps. ' Margot must have been astonished to have been forced to come back here,' she said with wry amusement. ' I wonder how Carlos persuaded her.'

Megan grinned. ' He didn't trouble to persuade her. He told her, just as he tells everyone what they are going to do! But he did bring me here, so that Margot would have somebody English to talk to— only, although he meant well, I don't think it was a very good idea from Margot's point of view.'

' No?' Señora Llobera sat bolt upright in her chair, looking considerably better. ' Are you not companionable to her?'

' I try to be, but she is not—not very—'

' Simpática?'

Megan flushed. ' It's my fault,' she said impulsively. ' I keep doing the wrong thing as far as she is concerned.'

' That is to be expected,' the old lady replied calmly. ' Come, my dear, I think it is time we joined the others!'

Megan had spent most of the afternoon setting the table and she couldn't help feeling a little thrill of pleasure as she saw the final results, with the candles lit and the bright colours of the anemones glowing in their warm light. Margot had invited the Navidades to join them after dinner; for the meal itself there was to be only the four of them, so as not to tire Señora Llobera too much.

The old lady was plainly enjoying herself. Her daughter might have had doubts about her eating so many varied rich foods late at night, the Señora herself had none! She sampled each dish with gusto, commenting on it with a frankness that Margot found embarrassing. Megan watched, amused, as Margot became more and more English as the evening progressed, driven out of her Spanish languor by the aristocratic manners of the real thing.

' What a good idea to eat early!' the old lady murmured, wondering whether to help herself to another helping of chicken.

' I thought you would prefer it,' Margot replied.

'I do! I have just said so! I have seldom eaten my evening meal before nine o'clock and by then I am never hungry. It is so stupid to keep to these absurd hours, don't you think?'

'I like to eat late,' Margot said in frigid tones.

'I remember my son-in-law saying that you did,' the old lady soothed her. 'I hear you are completely Spanish in your ways. When I was younger, I used to be less formal in my ways, but now I eat late and enjoy my *siesta*. As one grows older, one is forced to grow lazy, and our ways allow for this. The English are seldom lazy, I am told?'

Megan chuckled, earning for herself a glance of open dislike from her employer. 'We haven't the climate for it,' she said.

'Rubbish!' Margot exploded. 'It is entirely a matter of temperament. I have always felt completely at home in Spain proper!'

'But not in Mallorca?' the old lady teased her.

'I don't consider it truly Spanish. There are far too many tourists here for that!'

'I quite agree,' Señorita Anita put in unexpectedly. 'One hears English and German more often than Spanish nowadays!'

'In Soller?' her mother demanded with irony.

Señorita Anita looked discomfited. Megan felt sorry for her and, raising her chin belligerently, said, 'It's just as well as far as I'm concerned! My Spanish is frightful, but happily everyone speaks to me in English which I find very satisfactory.'

'Nevertheless, you will have to learn to speak good Spanish some time,' the old lady told her.

But Megan was barely listening. 'Why should I? I shan't need it when I go back to England, and I won't be here for long anyway.'

Everybody waited for the old lady to put her firmly in her place, but Señora Llobera only laughed. 'Perhaps Carlos will have something to say about that!'

she remarked.

'Carlos has already agreed to my going,' Megan said with dignity.

Margot nodded, pouring herself some more wine. 'He found it awkward when the Navidades stopped Inez coming here so often. I don't want to tell tales out of school, but they came to the conclusion that Megan was not an entirely suitable friend for her. Under the circumstances, Inez's interests come first with him, which is only proper.'

Megan hung her head miserably. She knew that Margot was right, but the truth left a bitter taste in her mouth. It had not been such a crime, surely, to have gone to the barbecue and to have sung in public. She felt the old lady watching her, but not even pride could make her feel anything but defeated.

'Señora de la Navidades says she is longing to hear Megan sing,' Señorita Anita said suddenly. 'She was telling me so yesterday. Apparently Inez was very impressed by how much everyone enjoyed her singing.' She turned to Megan. 'I hear you sing folk songs? Do you ever sing any Spanish songs?'

Megan shook her head. 'I'll learn one specially for you,' she promised.

'I'd like that,' Señorita Anita replied, with a fierce look round the table. 'You must come and visit us before you go and sing it to us.'

Megan hoped that Señora Llobera would confirm her daughter's invitation, but the old lady was busy talking to Margot about various mutual friends, having apparently lost all interest in Megan's affairs.

'I'll sing you something tonight,' Megan said rashly. 'And I'll sing it in Spanish!'

'How nice of you, my dear,' Señorita Anita exclaimed, very pleased.

But, when the Navidades had arrived with a great deal of noise, and Tony, looking sour and angry, had been brought upstairs by one of the maids, Megan wondered how she was going to fulfil her promise.

'Do you know any Spanish songs?' she asked Tony.

He looked at her from under glowering eyebrows. 'Should I?'

'Oh, Tony!' she sighed.

'I can't think why I came,' he went on. 'I never meant to! Much you care about any of us, Megan Meredith! One song you sang the other evening. *One song!* And then off you went, without a care in the world, leaving me to explain why you weren't singing again. That's the last time I ask you to do *anything* for me! The very last time! What's more, I'll see that none of my friends ever employ you back in England.'

'But, Tony, it wasn't my fault!'

'Oh, don't come the little girl with me!' he said unkindly. 'You're a big girl now, Megan. If you'd wanted to you could have stayed.'

'But I'm working for him—'

Tony shrugged his shoulders. 'That's your business. You might have explained at the beginning that he owned you and then I wouldn't have *embarrassed* you again!'

Megan winced. 'We can't fight here,' she whispered. 'Please, Tony!'

He picked up his guitar, still angry. 'You get away with murder, my love, sheer murder! Some day, someone will give you what for and the rest of us will raise a cheer. You've got it coming to you. I daresay this Spaniard is the very one for the job!'

Megan coloured. 'I told you, he's my employer!'

Tony gave her a sardonic smile. 'So you said, pet, so you said!'

'*But he is*—'

'Darling, if you go on protesting that he's *only* your employer, I'll never believe anything you say again.'

'But—' Megan shrugged, realising that she was

making too much of the whole thing. 'I'm sorry, Tony,' she said.

'You're forgiven, love. *This* time!'

'Oh, thank you, Tony!' Megan exclaimed gratefully.

'If you look at him like that, I'm not surprised he wants you all to himself,' Tony added, grinning. 'All guilty and falling over yourself to please!'

'I hope not!' Megan was horrified at the thought. 'It's just what he expects of women! But I'm not making myself a doormat for any man, certainly not for him!'

Tony gave her a quizzical look. 'More power to your elbow, love! I wish I could believe you. Now, supposing you tell me what you're going to sing?'

They agreed between them on two songs. The first was a traditional Spanish song, that was not too difficult to sing, with a rousing chorus that was all about the perils of wearing one's heart on one's sleeve when one's heart's delight was already dallying with another. It was a song that Megan sang with a tragic air and a self-mockery that was more appealing than she knew. When she had finished, she turned and smiled at Tony and was surprised to see that he had tears in his eyes. Her pulses leaped in triumph and with a sudden gamine grin, she went straight into the second song.

> *Spanish is the loving tongue,*
> *Soft as music, light as spray,*
> *'Twas a girl I learned it from,*
> *Living down Sonora way.*
> *I don't look much like a lover,*
> *Yet I say her loved words over often*
> *When I'm all alone:*
> *"Mi amor, mi corazon."* '

The silence of her audience made her smile as Tony struck a few chords to mark the end of one stanza and the beginning of the next. *My love, my heart!* She thought of Carlos and began to tremble inside. With a gulp, she began the second verse, blotting out all thought of him.

> 'Moonlight on the patio
> Old señora nodding near,
> Me and Juana talking low,
> So her madre couldn't hear.
> How the hours would go a-flying
> And too soon I'd hear her sighing
> In her sorry little tone,
> " Mi amor, mi corazon." '

Her voice died away, leaving the guitar to take over again. Megan sat, relaxed, waiting for the chord that would bring her in again, but that chord never came. There was a flurried noise outside the door and a flustered maid came running in and whispered a few words to Margot.

'It's Carlos!' Margot exclaimed. 'How could he come back tonight?' The impatience in her voice made them all look at her. Only Megan couldn't find it within herself to be surprised. She waited for the maid to whisk out of the room again and for the inevitable moment when Carlos would enter. But it was Pilar who came dancing in, still in her coat, delighted to be in Majorca again. She saw Megan immediately and embraced her fondly.

'You look just as pretty as I remember you!' she exclaimed generously. 'How lovely it is to see you again. I have been plying Carlos with questions about you all the way here, but he says nothing as always! Ay de mi, he is still the tirano odioso, that one!'

'Pilar!'

The Spanish girl turned immediately to her mother. 'Oh, how comfortable you are in this house now!' She kissed her mother lightly and shot off to greet Señora Llobera. 'How terrible of me not to see you before, señora. But of course you would be here to meet our charming Megan!'

The old lady allowed herself to be warmly kissed on either cheek. 'I see you talk as much as ever!' she rebuked the young girl, but she looked pleased all the same. 'Since when did Carlos become a tyrant, I should like to know?'

Pilar laughed gaily. 'Why, since he kidnapped Megan!' she answered cheerfully. 'I helped him,' she added, not without pride. Her eyes fell for an instant on Inez and she smiled at her a little uncertainly. 'Inez, how lucky that you are here! I have a message for you from Pepe!'

A babble of Spanish broke out as everyone began to talk to each other, exclaiming over Pilar's arrival, while she happily revelled in being the centre of attention.

'Where is Carlos?' Margot demanded, as soon as a certain order had been restored to her party.

'He's coming,' Pilar answered. 'We could hear Megan singing from the patio!' Her eyes danced wickedly. 'Perhaps he won't come in at all unless she sings for us some more. What will you sing, Megan? You will, won't you? Shall I accompany you, for I can you know!' She snatched Tony's guitar out of his hands and took up her stance beside Megan. 'You,' she informed him, 'can sit over there. You play like an Englishman, *amigo*, without any fire or spirit!'

'Oh, but—' Megan protested.

'It doesn't matter,' Tony cut across her. 'The whole family is in league against me!'

Pilar looked at him more closely. 'You are English! What are you doing here? I didn't think my mother knew any English people here?'

'Tony is a friend of Megan's,' Margot put in.

Pilar put a guilty hand to her mouth, her eyes dancing. 'Ah, now I know who you are! Oh, Megan, no wonder Carlos—'

' *Pilar!* ' Megan squealed.

Pilar looked suitably repentant. ' Are we waiting for Carlos?' she asked.

' No,' Megan said quickly.

Señora de la Navidade, whose English was not good enough to follow more than the gist of what everyone had been saying, spoke quickly to Inez and the Spanish girl came over to Megan.

' My mother wishes you to sing the song you sang— the other evening,' she said. ' I told her about it.'

' But I don't know it!' Pilar objected.

' It doesn't matter,' said Megan. ' I'll sing it without any accompaniment. In Ireland they often sing it that way.' She smiled briefly at Inez, feeling unaccountably guilty. ' Pilar exaggerates,' she added. ' Carlos has never been interested in me.'

Inez glowed, her mouth pouting a little with excitement. It would be a hard man who could resist her when she looked like that, Megan thought.

' Oh, that doesn't matter now!' Inez laughed casually. ' Pepe is coming home! Pepe is coming *here*!'

Megan gave her a look of complete confusion. ' You don't understand! Carlos didn't really kidnap me—'

Inez shrugged, still smiling. ' But of course he did!'

Megan's eyes met those of Carlos' grandmother across the room. The old lady sat, her back as straight as a poker, missing nothing of the undercurrents that swept round the room. She nodded, graciously granting Megan her permission to begin, imperiously beckoning to everyone else to sit down.

Megan had never felt less like singing. She tried to swallow the lump in her throat, concentrating on the sad, lilting Irish air. The words were poignant, words that she had always liked, but had never really understood until this moment. She would sing the song for Carlos, even if he wasn't listening, for it summed up her own condition almost exactly.

She launched into the first verse, her voice husky with the tears that were only just below the surface. She didn't dare look at her audience to see how they were receiving her performance. Instead, she looked down at her hands in her lap, wishing for the hundredth time that she had not been so young and silly as to fall in love with a man like Carlos Vallori Llobera.

She knew the instant that he came into the room. She refused to look at him, but she knew how he looked, standing in the doorway, tall and arrogant, his eyes angry and disapproving. She would have given anything not to have been singing at that moment, but she flung back her head and finished the song, because her pride wouldn't allow her to do anything else.

> ' *I'll wear stockings of silk*
> *And shoes of bright green leather*
> *Combs to buckle my hair*
> *And a ring for every finger.*

> ' *Feather-beds are soft*
> *And painted rooms are bonny,*
> *But I would trade them all*
> *For my handsome, winsome Johnny.*

> ' *Some say he's black*
> *But I say he's bonny;*
> *Fairest of them all*
> *Is my handsome, winsome Johnny.*

> ' *I know where I'm going,*
> *And I know who's going with me.*
> *I know who I love,*
> *But the dear knows who I'll marry.*'

She came to an abrupt finish, standing up with decision, bowing formally to her audience. Still she couldn't bring herself to look at Carlos. She knew he hadn't moved a muscle, but then nor had anyone else. They were sitting as if they had been carved from stone and she knew that in any other circumstances she would have considered that a triumph.

Then somebody did move. Tony left the chair where he had been sitting and caught her into his arms, kissing her on the cheek and then the lips.

'Darling, you've never sung it better!'

Megan froze, looking not at him, but over his shoulder to where Carlos was standing, his lips twisted in a cynical smile.

'You'll have to change the name to Tony the next time you sing it,' was all he said. 'It will make it all the more touching!' He turned to his grandmother, kissing her hand with all the elegance she had come to expect of him. 'If you are ready, *mia cara*, I'll drive you back to Soller.'

There was the usual flurry that accompanies the departure of guests at a party, complicated by the necessity for having to help Señora Llobera down the stairs to the patio. Pilar ran down the stairs after them, pulling at her brother's sleeve, but he shrugged her off, giving all his attention to his grandmother as he helped her into the front seat of his spacious car. Only when he had shut the rear door on his aunt and was getting into the driving seat himself did he look up at Pilar.

'Tell Megan I'll see her in the morning!' he commanded. And he drove off into the night without another word.

'I won't be here in the morning!' Megan reiterated stubbornly.

Margot, bored with the whole conversation, cast her a look of irritation. 'Where will you be?' she asked unfairly.

'Somewhere!' Megan claimed, more hurt than she

171

had believed was possible. 'Anywhere! I won't be summoned into his presence like a naughty child! How dare he send me such a message!'

'That's Carlos!' Margot said dryly.

Pilar glared at her mother. 'I don't suppose it's anything you've done,' she consoled Megan. He was anxious about his grandmother. The old lady looked fit to drop! I can't think why you invited her to come out late at night.' She hesitated, frowning. 'Why did you?' she threw at her mother.

'She wanted to hear the child sing,' Margot replied.

'Child!' Megan repeated. 'Child! That's all I hear from you all. I'm *not* a child. Her voice broke dangerously. 'In some ways I wish I were!'

Pilar gave her mother an ironic look. 'Couldn't you have made it a lunch party?'

Margot shook her head. 'I wanted Tony Starlight to be there.'

'Why?'

It was Megan who answered. She was moving restlessly round the room, wishing that it had been anyone but the triumphant Inez who had witnessed Carlos' humiliating indifference, followed by his even more humiliating summons for the morning.

'I can't accompany myself,' she said.

'But why ask *him*?' Pilar insisted.

Megan shrugged. 'He knows my style,' she answered indifferently. 'What does it matter? He doesn't mean anything!'

'I asked him to come,' Margot told her daughter. 'Pilar, you must be tired, my dear. Why don't you go to bed? It's typical of Carlos to upset us all when we were enjoying ourselves for once. I'm quite exhausted myself.'

'But you knew he was coming, Mother,' Pilar said, with that devastating frankness for which she was famous with her brothers and sisters. 'He told me he had told you when to expect us.'

'I don't remember,' said Margot.

'And why Tony Starlight?' Pilar insisted, ignoring Megan's pleading expression and scarlet face. 'Why him?'

'I've told you!' Megan exclaimed desperately.

A fleeting, tender smile flickered across Pilar's face. 'Well, Mother?'

'I thought it would be nice for Megan. She's used to a much freer and more social life than she has been living here!'

'And you wanted Carlos to see them together,' Pilar prompted her mother.

Margot looked suddenly angry. 'That too! Be your age, Pilar! If Carlos marries, it will be much better if he marries someone who understands *our* position! Someone like Inez—'

'Inez is frightened of him. She wants to marry Pepe.'

'Pepe is much too young to be thinking of such things!' Margot said sharply. 'Don't talk about things you know nothing whatsoever about, Pilar! I won't have it, and I won't be cross-questioned in this way. A couple of hours in Carlos' company and you think you can behave as he does! Well, you're *my* daughter, my girl, and I've heard quite enough from you for one day. You can, both of you, go to bed, and I hope you'll both be in a more reasonable frame of mind in the morning!'

Megan would have gone at once, but Pilar was made of sterner stuff. 'So that's it!' she stormed. '*Dios mio*, do you dislike Carlos so much?'

'It isn't a matter of liking or disliking anyone,' Margot retorted grimly. 'Don't you understand that *everything* was left to Carlos? If he marries someone like Inez, Señor de la Navidades will insist that he settles a proper amount on Pepe, you and Isabel, and on me too! The Spanish are realistic about family loyalties. Can you imagine someone like Megan doing anything for us? Oh no! She immediately set about reinforcing Carlos' obsession over his mother! It didn't take her long to discover that most of the money in the family is Llobera money! I thought the old Señora would make short work of her, she never did like the English—look at the way she treated me!—and one look at Tony Starlight should have been enough to tell her what sort of girl she is!' She laughed shortly. 'The old lady is more gullible than I thought! But Carlos had his eyes opened for once! He won't stop Megan going back to England now!'

'Oh, Mother!' Pilar sighed. Her mouth was white and pinched and, without her usual vivacity, she looked suddenly faded and older than her years. 'Oh, Mother!'

Megan felt cut off from them both, alone as she had never been alone before. Was it possible, she wondered without much interest, that Margot had engineered Tony's embrace as well? It seemed more than likely. He had been invited for that very purpose. She giggled, glad that her emotions had frozen into insensibility. The funny thing was that Tony had come out of the affair better than any of his detractors. He had been angry with her, but he had not been malicious. Nor had he patronised her, or tried to change her into something that she was not. Why, oh, why, if she had had to fall in love, hadn't she fallen in love with him? But she knew the answer to that, she thought drearily. She could say goodbye to Tony without a second thought, but now that she had to say goodbye to Carlos, it would be like tearing out her heart.

'Megan, you *must* see Carlos in the morning!' Pilar begged, the tears streaming down her face.

Megan turned and looked at her. She even smiled. 'I don't think I want to,' she said. And she went slowly up to her room, to the bed that Carlos had had as a small boy, pulling off her dress and allowing it to fall unheeded to the floor. From habit, she washed her face and cleaned her teeth, before she got into bed, pulled the bedclothes up over her head, and cried herself to sleep.

CHAPTER XII

Megan could hear Pilar and her mother arguing late into the night. She tried not to listen to their raised, angry voices, knowing that they were discussing her, but she couldn't have understood them anyway, for Pilar had lapsed into her native Spanish, which she found much easier than English. When at last they went to bed, Megan still couldn't sleep. She tossed restlessly back and forth, waiting for the dawn and the new day when she would go away from Carlos for ever.

It was nearly dawn when she heard him come in, banging the door behind him with a lack of consideration that was far from his usual manner. She lay, tense and scarcely daring to breathe, listening to his footsteps as he came up the stairs. She waited for him to go past her door, but he didn't. The footsteps paused and he rapped lightly on her door.

'Megan?'

'Go away!' she whispered back.

'*Amada*, my grandmother wishes for us to have lunch with her tomorrow—'

Megan pulled the bedclothes back over her head. '*Go away!*' she repeated.

He laughed shortly. 'Good night, *mi queridissima mujer!*'

Megan lay completely still, then she sat up suddenly. 'You've forgotten that I'm not a woman in your eyes! I'm still a child, to be laughed at, scolded and summoned into your presence whenever you're angry! You can't have it both ways, *señor!*'

He was silent for a long minute, until she thought he had gone away. Then he said, his voice very dry. 'Your Spanish is improving, *hija*, but then didn't I hear you say earlier that *Spanish is the loving tongue?*'

176

'Oh! Go away!' she snapped again.

His laughter rang unkindly in her ears. 'For now, my love,' he agreed. 'I'll see you in the morning. *Convenido?*'

But Megan refused to answer and, after a few minutes, he went away, whistling the tune of the folk song she had sung earlier, the sound of it mocking her as she tried to hate him. If she saw him again, she thought, he would persuade her to stay, and she couldn't stay, loving him as she did. He didn't love her, she knew that. If he did, he would have made sure that she knew it, and would have claimed her love in return. He was not an inexperienced, gauche teenager like herself! He knew what he was doing and what he wanted, and what he wanted obviously wasn't her! But then why, oh, why had he brought her here? The answer, she thought, had been staring her in the face all along. She was no more than a pawn in the long-standing feud between Carlos and his stepmother, to be used and then rejected as soon as she had served her purpose. They had both used her to hurt the other, without affection for her, or interest in her as a person. She hated them both! She even hated herself, for allowing them to make her feel cheap when Tony had kissed her. Why shouldn't he kiss her? At least he was genuinely fond of her!

The night crept by. When it was only just light, Megan pulled herself out of bed, refusing to give way to the weariness that engulfed her, and dressed, defiantly, in a mauve tweed trouser suit. She had only one thought and that was to get away from the house, and anything that reminded her of Carlos, until she could find a travel agent and buy a ticket on the next plane to London. She wondered how much it would cost, and felt very sorry for herself when she thought of the lonely homeward journey and compared it with the comfort of travelling with Carlos on the way out.

The only thing to do was to get as far away as

possible before anyone else got up. She hurried downstairs, carrying her shoes in her hand in case anyone heard her moving about, trying to make up her mind where she should hide until the plane went. She hadn't really come to any decision when she let herself out of the patio into the street, but when she found herself looking at Margot's car she didn't hesitate. She got into the driving seat, found the ignition key in the front pocket, and drove off down the street. Margot, of course, would not be pleased to find her car gone, and without her permission, but Megan didn't care. She felt curiously light-headed and unlike herself.

She took the motorway out of Palma, not caring where she went, driving on and on into the rising sun. The almond blossom went unnoticed and she barely saw the towns that she went through, until she realised that she was completely lost, without the slightest idea of which way she should go next. Not that it mattered, she reminded herself with a sob. Who cared where she was? Or what she did?

A signpost told her that she was near the sanctuary of San Salvador, which she thought she had read something about, though she couldn't remember what. She turned up the narrow road that led to the foot of a massive hill, the sole peak that rose some fifteen thousand feet above the surrounding plain. No one, she thought, would think of looking for her there— if they were looking for her, which she very much doubted.

The road wound upwards, climbing steadily to the top where a handful of monks still lived in the ancient hermitage, earning their living in the modern restaurant they had built there, with its fantastic view right across the south of the island.

Megan parked the car and sauntered through the buildings, peering into the church and browsing through the memorials and tokens of thanksgiving that hung, in the way that they do in much of the continent, in a chapel dedicated to San Salvador. The faded photographs of sailors lost at sea, children dead before their time, and the promises of pilgrimages to be made and prayers to be said in return for favours received, fitted in with her mood of forlorn unhappiness. Afterwards, she went out into the sunshine again, studied the splendid view and the prickly pear with moody interest, and wondered what she should do next.

The car sailed down the road to the bottom of the hill, almost without her having to do anything at all. At the bottom, she took a last look at the statue at the top, that stood overlooking the plain, blessing all that came and went past the ancient hermitage.

As she paused to turn into the main road again, she thought she saw Carlos' car going fast in the opposite direction. Her heart knocked against her ribs and her hands trembled on the steering wheel. He was looking for her! Supposing he were to find her? She couldn't bear it if he argued with her, worse, *disapproved* of her again. She tore out into the road, almost colliding with a horse and cart that she hadn't even seen. The driver yelled an insult at her and Megan offered a fleeting apology, putting her foot right down on the accelerator and allowing the car to rip up the road ahead of her in sheer panic in case Carlos should be following her.

She had reached Porto Cristo before she had pulled herself together sufficiently to slow down and make some effort to drive properly. There was nowhere now to go, except into the sea, and she stopped the car, brushing the tears out of her eyes, jumping as each car went past her, sure that it would be Carlos, angry and menacing, behind the wheel.

A coach, full of waving tourists, pulled out to pass her and she slowed almost to a stop to let it go. But it did not go on down the hill into Porto Cristo.

Instead it turned off into what looked like a picnic area, well-wooded, and showing the signs of any much visited place. Megan followed the coach very slowly, allowing it to get well ahead of her. She saw then that she had arrived at the Cuevas de Drach and remembered the Englishwoman's enthusiasm at the barbecue. Of course, she thought, she had come to the Dragon's Cave.

She might not have gone in. She bought a ticket largely by accident, thinking that she was only asking how much the ticket was. The man took her purse from her, counted out the right number of pesetas and put the ticket in her hand, telling her not to lose it, for it would be more than half an hour before the next batch of visitors could be taken down to the caves.

There was a short walk to the entrance, crowded with tourists of all nationalities, and Megan walked along it with the rest of them, turning her head every now and again, almost as if she expected someone to be following her. She saw Carlos long before he saw her. He was asking the man at the ticket office if he had seen her. His description of her brought forth a voluble and enthusiastic discourse, assuring him that she would not yet have gone into the caves, but that, if he hurried, he could easily catch her up. Megan knew exactly what was being said, just as though she could hear and understand every word. But she had eyes only for Carlos' face, and it was every bit as angry and menacing as she had imagined it would be.

She turned and ran. A few steps led down to the caves below and she hurtled down them, almost throwing her ticket at the guardian who was vainly trying to gather his group of tourists together before they made their descent.

'*Señorita!*' he called after her. She looked back and smiled at him when he shrugged his shoulders and let her go on. She almost fell down the last few steps as she met the warm, wet atmosphere of the caves and felt the crush of the tourists coming on behind her. She felt safe then. There were so many of them, building an insurmountable barrier between herself and Carlos. She took a deep breath of relief, sure that he couldn't possibly have seen her, and began to look about her at the glories of the most spectacular caves in an island of caverns and hollow hills.

Perhaps it was because they progressed so slowly that Megan found her feet dragged along the rough path and up and down the steps that led from one brilliantly lit cavern to the next. The hanging stalactites, known as the hanging pins, intrigued her. They were small and delicate by comparison with some of the great columns that went between roof and floor in magnificent shapes, fashioned over who knew how many thousands of years. Somebody exclaimed over a stalagmite that resembled a hooded monk, and she herself was entranced by the clarity of the water in what was known as ' Diana's Baths '.

It grew hotter as they went along. Megan supposed it was the hot breath of countless tourists that made the atmosphere so close. Her trousers clung to her damp legs and her eyes felt gritty from lack of sleep, However long did it take to walk through these caves? She should have enquired, she thought. She didn't want Carlos to be waiting at the exit when she finally surfaced back into the fresh air.

Then, just as she was beginning to despair, they reached the final and largest cave, which had been turned into a theatre. Rows and rows of wooden forms had been bolted to the floor, facing the lit up underground Lake Martel. Megan would have gone on, forgoing the concert in an effort to get out of the caves and away before Carlos could catch up with her, but the attendant ushered her brusquely into a seat on the far side of the makeshift auditorium. She sat down reluctantly on the wooden form, sliding along it until she came up against a bar that was the only barrier between her and the water below. Someone sat down beside her with a faint smile of apology, and the auditorium slowly filled up with laughing and chattering tourists. Megan's eyes searched up and down the rows, looking for Carlos, but he wasn't there. She slouched down in her seat, more miserable even than before, wondering why it wasn't relief that she was feeling.

The lights went down and they sat in darkness. The bright red of a moving pinpoint of light told her that someone was smoking despite the various notices asking one not to. Everyone waited in silence, their conversations cut short except for the occasional, excited whisper, and then the music began, a slow murmur of violins that grew gradually louder.

Megan was hardly aware of the movement beside her. Her neighbour moved away from her and someone else slipped into the vacated seat beside her.

' Hullo, Megan,' he said.

It was Carlos.

She sat as far away from him as was humanly possible, the wooden bar biting into her ribs. It didn't make any difference. He sat a little closer to her, his thigh tight against hers, a hand on her far shoulder, pulling her closer still.

' *Déjeme!* ' she whispered in Spanish. ' Oh, Carlos, please leave me alone! '

' Not until you promise you won't run away again,' he answered her. ' I've spent a wretched morning following you around this island and I don't intend to spend the better half of the afternoon doing the same thing! '

' You can't,' she reminded him. ' You're having lunch with your grandmother! '

' *We* are having lunch with her,' he retorted. ' You and I together—'

' It's too late to go there now,' she objected.

He grinned, and she could see his teeth shining white in the darkness. 'My grandmother is very Spanish, *mi corazon*. She won't expect us much before three.'

Slowly, from behind an island column in the middle of the lake, a boat slipped into view, outlined in tiny lights. The music swelled, taking a light-hearted turn, and another boat followed and then another, dancing with each other in the darkness in time to the music. It was just possible to make out the dark shapes of the men who were playing the music in the first boat as it glided by, quite close to them. In the other boats there was only the oarsman, his movements kept to a minimum as he soundlessly dipped his oar into the gleaming water.

The music changed and the audience, recognising the tune, began to hum, swaying in time to the music. It was a moment of sweetness that would linger with Megan all her life, bound up as it was with the hard feel of Carlos beside her, and the tang of his after-shave lotion in her nostrils as he bent his head to hers.

She had not meant to allow him to kiss her. She shut her eyes when his lips met hers and, when she opened them again, the boat carrying the musicians had gone out of sight and the music had changed again.

'I won't!' Megan whispered indignantly, just as he kissed her again.

The feel of his laughter made her heart pound within her. She held back for as long as she could and then, with a gesture of surrender, she put a hand on his shoulder and gave herself up to the agonising ecstasy of his kiss. It wouldn't hurt Inez—or anyone!—if she had that to remember for the rest of her life.

The lights came on slowly and Megan pulled herself away from Carlos, startled by the audience about her coming to life. The boats had already waltzed their

way round to the back of the column and out of sight.
The performance was over.

Megan leapt to her feet, hurrying over more tardy
feet than her own with a muttered apology here and
there. Carlos caught her by the hand and pulled her
back against him, forcing her to slow down.

'Carlos, leave me alone!'

'*Ni hablar!*'

'I—I don't understand.'

He chuckled. 'You wouldn't, it wasn't a term of
endearment. I said, not on your life!'

'It isn't fair!' Megan protested. 'Carlos, let's get
out of here. I'm going back to England and that's
that! *Everyone* will be pleased!'

'Everyone?'

'Everyone. Margot and—and Inez—'

'And you?'

'Oh, Carlos, that isn't a fair question!' Her voice
broke and she swallowed desperately to keep from
crying.

'Isn't it, *pequeña*? But can't you see that it all
depends on that?'

Megan wiped her face with the back of her hand,
hoping that he wouldn't notice in the poor lighting.
'Oh, look!' she bade him. 'Isn't—isn't the water
clear down there?'

He looked down to where she was pointing with
complete indifference. 'Last time I came, this path
wasn't here,' he told her. 'It took much longer to
come out. Judging by the change of atmosphere,
we're nearly there.' He took her hand in his, to help
her up the last flight of stairs, running his thumb
over the dampness that was all that was left of her
tears. 'The prospect of going back to England doesn't
seem to have made you very happy, *hija*,' he remarked.

The slow-moving group came to a complete halt.
Megan looked over her shoulder, her eyes meeting
Carlos' ironic gaze fleetingly.

'You don't understand!' she began.

'What don't I understand?'

'Why I have to go away. You should never have brought me here in the first place! Poor Inez! I feel quite sorry for her—' She turned away, gulping in the cool air from above. 'You aren't *kind* to anyone!'

'Am I supposed to have some particular obligation to be kind to Inez?' he enquired, moving up a step so that she could feel his long, hard body close up against hers. 'Inez is Pepe's girl. They are a good match for each other. At least, she doesn't start like a frightened rabbit every time she sees him!'

'But—'

'*Dios mio*, Megan! *Qué disparate!* How could you suppose that Inez would hold any interest for me? Didn't I tell you right at the beginning that I am a man, that the boy that was me no longer existed? What would I do with Inez? She would be frightened half to death!'

'She is a year older than I am,' Megan pointed out.

His eyes glinted dangerously. 'Is that so?' he drawled. 'And were you frightened half to death when I kissed you?'

Megan blushed. 'No,' she said simply. She didn't want to remember what she had felt when he had kissed her. If she did, she knew she would never gather enough courage to leave him, no matter how urgent her reasons for going.

'That's what I thought!' His hand caressed the back of her neck beneath the curtain of her hair. 'What happened, that now you want to run away?'

Her knees felt weak and she drove herself to the edge of anger so that she wouldn't give way to the delicious feel of his hands. 'What happened?' she repeated. 'You know what happened! How dared you be so contemptuous yesterday! What if Tony did like my singing, and you didn't? You could at least have said hullo!'

His hand tightened on her neck. 'If I had said anything to you just then, I would have slapped you!'

She shivered, thankful that they were on the move again. 'It wasn't my fault,' she said defensively. 'I didn't want him to kiss me.'

'That wasn't the way it looked to me.' He gave her a little shake, making her stumble and miss her step. 'In future, my girl, you can keep all your kisses for me, no matter how much you feel like flirting with someone else!'

The sheer injustice of this bereft her of speech. She made a last dash up the steps, past a stall selling postcards and various souvenirs and guides, and out into the sunshine, with Carlos in hot pursuit.

'Now what's the matter?' he roared at her.

Megan stopped, very much on her dignity. 'I do not flirt!' she informed him with a toss of her head.

He came level, catching up her hand in his. 'You flirt; you tell lies; and you're so young that I have no peace thinking about you. I imagine that you think you are in love with this Tony of yours. I spend hours telling myself that you are so free with him merely because you are English and have had a different upbringing from the Spanish girls I know. I even suspect that you wish to see him to annoy me, to find out how far you can go before my patience is exhausted and I make sure that you know you are mine once and for all! But you are young and I must give you time to find yourself! Well, you have no more time, *mi queridissima mujer!* Your growing up is done, so you may as well make up your mind to spending your life with me, whether you like it or not, and that your kisses are mine, and that, if you have to flirt, you can flirt with me!'

Her eyes opened very wide. 'Did you call me your darling woman?' she asked inconsequently.

'Ah!' he grunted. 'I might have known that you

would understand that!'

A glimmer of a smile came into her eyes. 'It isn't in my phrase book,' she said.

'I imagine that it wouldn't be very useful to the average tourist!' he retorted.

'I don't know,' she murmured. 'The Spanish are said to be very hot-blooded.' She grinned provocatively. 'I suppose that's why you find it necessary to closet your daughters. I prefer my independence!'

'What a pity you will have it for such a short while!' he drawled.

Megan blushed. She turned and walked away to where she had left the car.

'Meganita, where are you going now?' he called after her.

She was shaken by his use of her name, and she longed to tell him that his grandmother, too, had called her Meganita, and how much they had liked each other.

'I must take Margot's car back to Palma,' she said. She looked at him doubtfully, taking in his harassed expression and the wild disorder of his hair. Had she done that, she wondered, when he had kissed her in the dark of the cave? 'I—I didn't ask her if I could borrow it.'

His grasp on her wrist tightened, pulling her towards him. 'It is of no importance,' he said firmly. 'You are coming with me!'

'I'm not!' She wished he wouldn't look at her in quite that way, and that she didn't feel so weak at the knees. 'I have to take the car back. And then I'm going to buy my ticket! Carlos, are you listening to me?'

His arms went right round her and she thought he was going to kiss her. She shut her eyes, willing him to do so. 'C-Carlos?' she repeated.

'Don't try your tricks on me!' he accused her angrily. 'You're coming with me! Understand?'

'Yes, Carlos.'

He glanced at her, suspicious of this unexpected meekness. 'Megan, I have to talk to you first. If I kiss you now, I won't be able to stop, and then we will be late for lunch.'

'I don't care.'

His expression grew arrogant, his frown shadowing his dark green eyes. 'So,' he said, his voice as cold as steel, 'the thought of being kissed by me doesn't frighten you any more?'

'I've never been frightened of you!' she claimed.

'Oh, Megan!' he mocked her.

She chewed at her lower lip thoughtfully, wishing that she could behave in a cool, calm, *adult* way, with Carlos at her feet, hanging on her every word, instead of ordering her around and making her do everything *his* way!

'I may have been surprised,' she went on, 'but certainly not frightened!'

He laughed. 'Oh, Megan, I do love you!'

'Do you?' The urgency behind the question shocked her. She tried to escape his restraining hands. 'I mean—I mean, you've kissed a lot of people, haven't you?'

'A few,' he agreed soberly.

'There you are, then,' she concluded. 'You might kiss someone, but it doesn't mean anything, does it? It—it doesn't make that person any more *suitable*—'

He smiled straight into her eyes. 'I don't think any of them were *surprised*,' he teased her. 'And they were all of them quite suitable for the moment!'

She winced, trying once again to escape him. 'But I'm not suitable,' she pointed out. 'I tried to do what you wanted while you were away, and I couldn't even do that. Your family don't think me suitable at all!'

He opened the door of his car and pushed her in. Megan subsided on to the front seat, looking defeated and weary after her sleepless night. He shut the door on her and walked round the car, getting in beside her. He spent a long moment, silently looking at her, until she grew restive and pulled at the creases of her trouser legs, wishing that she had worn a skirt after all.

' My family will accept the woman of my choice,' he said. ' They are not important—'

' They are important! They're very important—to me!'

' Then they will welcome you,' he answered grimly.

She shook her head. ' Not even you can force them to do that. Carlos, don't you see? Margot doesn't like me, and she's afraid for the future. Didn't your father leave her any money of her own?'

' He had little enough to leave. He lived on my mother's money from the moment they were married.'

' Was that why he married her?' Megan asked in a small voice.

' Very likely!' Carlos agreed dryly.

' Your grandmother said your mother was bored and restless,' Megan went on bravely. ' You're very like her—'

' Are you afraid that you might bore me?'

She bit her lip. ' N-no,' she said.

His eyebrows lifted and he looked amused. ' Then, as there is no possibility of my marrying you for your money, why do you still wish to run away?'

Megan wriggled with embarrassment, looking every bit as young as her eighteen years. ' You haven't asked me not to go,' she reminded him.

' Nor will I! You know very well why I brought you to Mallorca, Megan. I shan't prevent you if you want to go. I seem to remember that Tony Starlight asks your permission before he kisses you. If that is what you prefer—' The cynical twist to his mouth cut through her embarrassment, bringing home to her the astonishing fact that he wasn't as sure of himself as she had supposed. The knowledge brought a leap to her pulses and an effervescent sense of power that went to her head like wine.

'Tony kisses very nicely,' she remarked, not looking at him.

Carlos laughed harshly. 'I'll give you something to compare his kisses with!' he shot at her. He reached over for her and yanked her along the seat towards him, ignoring her cry of protest as her knee knocked against the gear lever. His lips closed over hers in a kiss that hurt her mouth. With a little sob, her arms went round his neck and she eased herself closer to him. 'Oh, Carlos,' she whispered, 'I thought you were never going to kiss me again!'

'Wishful thinking, *hija*!' he whispered. His hand slid under her coat and tore at her blouse. 'No,' he said at last. 'I think we had better behave ourselves. I will drive you over to a pleasant, respectable lunch with my grandmother, and after that, I'll take you home and break the news to Margot and Pilar that you are going to marry me as soon as I can arrange it—'

Megan smiled at him. 'You haven't asked me yet,' she complained.

'I'm not going to!' he retorted. 'And don't look at me like that, or I shall kiss you again, and if I touch you again I shan't be answerable for the consequences!'

She chuckled. 'Darling!'

His eyes lit with mocking amusement. 'You must learn to say it in Spanish,' he told her.

'Mmm,' she agreed. 'Spanish is the loving tongue.' She hesitated, suddenly shy. '*Amado*,' she experimented, rolling the word off her tongue.

'*Alma mia!*' he responded.

'*Mi corazon*, my heart, I love you very much,' she whispered. Her eyes darkened with emotion. 'How soon can we be married?' she asked him.

'If you go on looking at me like that it had better be soon,' he answered ruefully. 'I am not sure your Tony wouldn't be a more suitable husband for you, he added thoughtfully. 'He is English like yourself—'

Megan reached up and kissed him on the lips. 'I'm tired of hearing about Tony,' she complained. 'Nor do I want you to ask my permission before you kiss me.' The ready colour ran up into her cheeks. 'I want you to take them, because they're all yours, if—if you want them?'

'My dearest beloved,' he answered, 'why else do you suppose I brought you to Mallorca? You were mine from the first moment I saw you!'

'In the Witch's Cauldron?' she said, surprised.

'Singing some spell that bound me to you,' he accused her, laughing. 'My only defence was a poor little dragon whose breath was supposed to frighten you into my arms.'

'Perhaps that's why I came to his cave,' she said idly. She looked suddenly anxious. 'Carlos, I'm not too young for you, am I? I'll try to be everything you wish me to be, but be patient with me, and love me, even when I annoy you and you want to—to slap me!'

He kissed her hard on the mouth and then put her firmly away from him, his hands trembling slightly as he started up the engine.

'You are everything I want,' he said. 'Everything. For you, my sweet, I'll buy off Margot and let her go to England, if that's what she wants to do. And I'll give Pilar and the others whatever they want. But you, *alma mia*, will stay with me wherever I am and give me what *I* want, whether you like it or not, because I can't do without you!'

Megan tucked her left hand into the crook of his arm, loving him with her eyes. With her other hand she buttoned up her coat and smoothed down her trousers over her legs. 'Yes, Carlos,' she said demurely. And they laughed delightedly together.

Each month from Harlequin

8 NEW FULL LENGTH ROMANCE NOVELS

ALL BOOKS 60¢

These titles are available at your local bookseller, or through the Harlequin Reader Service, M.P.O. Box 707, Niagara Falls, N.Y. 14302; Canadian address 649 Ontario St., Stratford, Ont.

R